A LITTLE BIT
Wicked

A FORBIDDEN LOVE NOVEL

A LITTLE BIT
Wicked

A FORBIDDEN LOVE NOVEL

ROBYN DEHART

Entangled Publishing, LLC
2614 South Timberline Road
Suite 109
Fort Collins, CO 80525
Visit our website at www.entangledpublishing.com.

Scandalous is an imprint of Entangled Publishing, LLC.

Edited by Alethea Spiridon Hopson
Cover Design by Heidi Stryker

ISBN 978-1-943892-41-9

Manufactured in the United States of America

First Edition December 2012

For M & Z, you have changed my life in amazing ways. I love being your mommy.

And as always for Paul, my soul mate and the best daddy since my own.

Prologue

Vivian March checked again to make certain her mask was secured in place. This was only her second masked ball since she'd come out four years before and she wasn't used to the tickle of feathers and velvet against her cheeks. Excitement thundered through her body, setting her nerves on edge.

Tonight was the night, and she wanted him to know how very thrilled she was at the prospect, which was why she'd snuck out to the gardens to see him. But she also intended to do something scandalous. It wasn't proper for a lady to kiss a gentleman, even if they were engaged, but tonight she wanted to be brazen—wicked, even. She smiled in the darkness. It was not as though she hadn't been truly wicked in his arms already.

Not only had she finally met the man she would marry, but it was a love match. They were the lucky ones. Love matches were rare indeed, but especially for a woman such as herself, at the ripe age of four and twenty. She had had her come-out late, having not been introduced into society until she'd turned twenty. The first three Seasons were spent dancing with plenty of gentlemen, but she realized quickly that men were only interested in her because of her sizeable inheritance.

And then she had met Frederick, her sweet and passionate Frederick. He had changed everything.

She left the noise and lights of the ballroom and made her way out to the terrace that would lead her to the gardens. They were to meet at a quarter of eleven and she still had about five minutes before their secret rendezvous. The pebbles on the path crunched beneath her dancing slippers, but the discomfort only heightened her awareness, reminded her how reckless her behavior was. These slippers were delicate and lovely, but meant for ballroom dancing only, not a rendezvous in the garden. But Vivian ignored all of that because she was made of sturdier stuff.

A few couples walked arm-in-arm past her. They too were out enjoying the bright night with the full moon illuminating the gardens. Vivian kept moving. She forced herself to walk instead of running into the garden, so eager was she. They were to meet by the willow trees near the pond.

As she made her way down the gently sloping hill, she saw the pond up ahead and a gentleman's tall frame standing near the water's edge. Even from behind, she could tell he looked positively dashing, dressed all in black. He didn't see her approach, and she stepped quietly so as not to alert him. She wanted to surprise him. Her heart pounded and happiness threatened to choke her. Oh, how she loved that man! She sent another thank you heavenward for her good fortune. She moved as quickly and as quietly as she could until she'd reached him. Without another thought, she flung herself against him, snaked her arms around his neck, and kissed him with all the passion and love she felt.

Strong, masculine arms came around her and his kiss deepened. The kiss felt different this time, more passionate, more heady, more intense somehow. Desire poured through her, threatening to weaken her knees, so she clung more tightly to him. Perhaps this new awareness stemmed from what had transpired between them since their first kiss. And tonight she would become his in the eyes of London.

He ended the kiss and held her out in front of him. "Brazen and delectable," he said.

Vivian's heart fell to her stomach. That was *not* Frederick's voice. She reached up and ripped off the man's domino mask. Definitely not Frederick. Her mouth fell open.

He smiled, a crooked smile that transformed him into a most dashing man. He was young, perhaps only twenty, perhaps younger, but so handsome with that cocky smile and blue eyes that seared her.

She had kissed him. A stranger.

And not merely a simple, sweet kiss, but rather a deep, passionate, open-mouthed kiss. She prayed for a hole to open in the ground and swallow her up, but alas, two breaths later she was still standing there, as was he, still wearing that charming yet annoying grin.

He reached over and removed her mask. "That was quite an introduction. I can assure you, I won't forget you anytime soon." He bowed dramatically. "Marcus Kincaid."

"Vivian March," she said out of polite habit, and then realized she probably should have kept that piece of information to herself. "You must understand," she continued, "that I thought you were someone else. That kiss—" she shook her head. "That was not intended for you. I am most apologetic, not to mention thoroughly embarrassed."

He shrugged. "Don't be. It's the best thing that's happened to me all evening." He clicked his tongue. "Pity all that passion was intended for someone else, though." His eyes traveled the length of her. "He's a lucky fellow."

"I do hope you will be kind and keep this—" She searched for the appropriate word. "—misunderstanding to yourself. Forget you ever met me."

"That would be unlikely. I shall keep your little secret, but I won't forget you or that kiss." He turned on his heel. "Good evening, Miss March."

She watched him walk away, and released a slow breath. Her shoulders slumped. Where was Frederick? Certainly it was past the time of their arranged meeting. Had something happened to him?

Oh no. Had he seen her in the arms of another man and fled? A wave of nausea passed through her. How would she explain, if he'd seen her kissing another man? She waited for several more minutes, pacing at the water's edge, before finding her way back to the ballroom. The wall clock pronounced it eleven-thirty. Where was he?

Forty minutes later she entered the front door of her townhouse. She found her two aunts sitting in the front parlor playing cards, clearly waiting up for her, as normally they did not stay up this late.

"Did you have a nice time, dear?" Aunt Lillian asked.

"What? Oh yes, it was a lovely time," Vivian said. She hadn't told them about her and Frederick's plans for the evening. She had wanted to surprise them. They'd had such hopes for her when she'd first come out, and then those years had passed without even a hint of a proposal. All three of them had begun to lose hope, though they'd never said as much. Vivian could tell they worried she would end up like them—spinsters, wealthy, and alone.

"You received this note shortly after you left for the ball," Aunt Rose said. She turned the note over in her hand, and held it out to Vivian. "Looks to be from that painter fellow."

Vivian's heart seemed to stop beating and her breathing became shallow. If he'd sent the note right after she'd left for the ball, then perhaps he hadn't seen her kissing another man. She took the note and cracked the wax seal.

My dearest Vivian,

I know you are probably waiting for me tonight and I hate that I cannot be there with you. Please know that what I am doing, I do for us. I am leaving for Paris to study with the masters so that I can become the very best artist I can be. I know that your fortune is enough for both of us and I have money from my family, but I want to provide for you myself. Make my own fortune. I shall return for you and we can marry then. I love you, my dearest.

Yours forever,
Frederick Noble

The letter fell from her hand. Vivian vaguely heard her aunts talking, but their voices blurred into the distance. The only thought she had before she fell to the floor was that she had trusted him, given him her heart, and her body, and he had left her.

And now she was ruined.

Chapter One

His brother was dead, and damnation if he hadn't missed the funeral. And not by a couple of days, but rather several months. Evidently, no one had seen fit to send him notice.

Marcus Kincaid poured himself a third glass of brandy and swore loudly. He glanced around the late earl's study, noting the meticulous arrangement of furniture—the tidy stack of papers on the desk, the quill in its holder, and the inkwell free from any drips or stains. He doubted anyone had been in here since his brother's passing. It was as if the entire room had been set up as a shrine.

Marcus slammed his glass onto the desk, sloshing the contents onto an envelope. His brother's name and address smeared and bubbled until only a black puddle of ink remained.

He took a deep breath and briefly closed his eyes. He stepped away from the desk, making his way to the wingback chair across the room. Halfway there he stopped and looked at the globe. Marcus scoffed, spun the miniature world, and watched it slow to a few restless circles. He plopped his finger onto the ball and stopped it.

Africa. His latest tour had been Africa, where he'd given England's wealthiest citizens the bloody adventure of their lifetimes. All the while, his own brother had died of something no more exciting than a lung infection. Granted, Charles had been more than fifteen years his senior, still Marcus hadn't been prepared for his death. The Kincaids had seen more than their fair share of deaths.

He dropped into the chair. He couldn't help noticing it was more comfortable than any place he'd sat or slept during his entire trek through Africa. The guests traveling with Thomas Adventure Tours slept in lavish tents with plush bedding while the guides were relegated to more inferior quarters. He hadn't minded much, though. He'd enjoyed his work—lived for it, if he were honest.

He tilted back his head and stared at the ceiling. The ornate wood carving at the top of the chair dug into his scalp. He pushed his head against it, increasing the dull pain.

The death of his older brother, the Earl of Ashford, meant one thing—now *he* was the bloody earl. Marcus searched his body for feelings of grief, but felt only numbing shock. They'd never had the traditional sibling relationship, he and Charles. The eldest Kincaid son had been raised to be the heir, raised to run the properties, and expected to serve in Parliament. And he'd been nearly sixteen when Marcus had been born. By the time he'd learned to read, Charles had been married.

Upon his return to England, Marcus had come home to

Ashford Hall fully expecting to see things much as he'd left them. Instead, he'd found his Aunt Maureen had moved in to be the full-time guardian to his younger sister Clarissa, and the entire house had been shrouded in mourning.

"It's fortunate that you chose this week to return," Aunt Maureen said as she floated into the room. She was a formidable woman with a large frame, yet she managed to maneuver herself with surprising grace.

"Yes, fortunate was precisely what I was thinking," he said, doing nothing to hide the sarcasm in his voice.

"The Season hasn't even opened yet and technically we have a couple more months of mourning, but your sister has managed to get herself into quite the predicament." Maureen lowered herself onto the leather sofa adjacent to his chair. She had hinted about something dire she needed to speak with him about when he'd arrived the night before, but she'd allowed him time to rest.

Evidently, his resting time had ended. "Yes, you mentioned something last night."

"If we don't take action soon," she said, "there will be a terrible scandal—one from which she might not ever recover."

"Certainly it cannot be that bad." He pinched the bridge of his nose, willing the dull headache away. "It is not as if the girl has gotten herself compromised."

"Not quite," Maureen said holding up one finger. "But we were not far from that."

Marcus swore, then shook his head in lieu of apologizing. "What happened?"

"She was seen speaking to a questionable gentleman." It was on his tongue to wave her off. That alone was not so scandalous.

"Outside of his gaming hell."

He swore again. "What the devil was she thinking?"

"She claims to have had business to discuss with him and will say nothing more on the matter."

"What manner of business could a girl possibly have with a man the likes of him?"

"She is hardly a girl anymore," Maureen said. "She is three and twenty."

How was it possible that Clarissa was already a fully grown woman? Of course he'd seen her briefly when he'd arrived the night before, but he hadn't stopped to think about it. He hadn't expected a lot upon his return. Primarily, he hadn't expected his brother would be gone.

Over and over he kept realizing that he was now the earl. *He* was in charge of this family. Charles had always handled family matters with a deft, but firm, hand. Marcus considered what Charles would have done in this situation. For one thing, he would not allow the girl to remain secretive about her goings-on.

Marcus sat up, bracing his elbows on his knees. "I want her down here now to answer my questions." He pointed to the carpet for added emphasis. Then he stood. No, Charles would not wait on anyone. "Never mind. I shall go to her and demand answers."

Marcus ran up the stairs with his aunt trailing somewhere behind. He stormed into his sister's room. She jumped at the intrusion. Clarissa stood before her writing desk, where she'd been sitting and penning a letter.

"What are you about, barging into my private rooms?" she asked. Her brow knitted in a tense frown.

"I demand to know the truth of what happened at this

gaming establishment," he said. Yes, that is how Charles would have approached this. He would not have asked; he would simply have expected to receive the information.

Her eyes flared and she stepped over to him. "You demand? You have no right to demand!" She settled her hands on her hips. "You haven't been part of this family since I was thirteen. You might be the earl now, but I have been living on my own, with Aunt Maureen, of course." She motioned toward their aunt standing behind him. "And without any man to keep me protected. We've managed perfectly well on our own."

"You're embroiled in a scandal. If ever you needed a man's protection, it's now."

"I don't want your protection," she said, crossing her arms over her chest. Her features set, her eyes staring straight at him as if daring him to defy her.

Charles would know precisely what to do in this situation, know how to calm Clarissa and know how to squelch the rumors. Marcus knew precisely where to shoot a lion to stop him cold from attacking an unsuspecting Englishman. He knew how to use a knife to protect a group of travelers from a spitting cobra. He knew how to tie a hundred different knots and build a fire with nothing more than flint and a handful of brush. But he knew virtually nothing about his own sister or how to manage his new familial responsibilities.

He did, however, know when to retreat from a foe he couldn't possibly battle. Marcus turned and stepped out of Clarissa's bedchamber. Arguing with her was getting them nowhere. He needed to reassess. Come up with a different plan.

Clarissa slammed the door behind him. Marcus glanced

at Maureen.

She gave him a smile. "Pardon me, nephew, for my boldness, but you barely know your sister. You left when she was but a child and you've been gone since she was but a child. You cannot simply barge in there and demand answers." Maureen took a slow breath. "Might I suggest an alternative?"

Marcus eyed her, then nodded slowly.

"I know someone who can help." Maureen tapped her fingers on the wood paneling that lined the upstairs corridor. "Someone who will be better equipped to persuade Clarissa to talk—someone who might assist in smoothing over the situation. Perhaps even make it disappear altogether."

"I'm not certain we need to bring anyone else in on this. Our goal is to keep the situation quiet, is it not?"

"I wasn't actually asking you for permission," Maureen said. "I have, in fact, already contacted this person."

"Well, you can contact them again. Tell them we are not in need of their services," he said. He was not so archaic that he didn't believe women were allowed their opinions, but he had had enough of the women in his family telling him how things were going to be. He might have been gone for the better part of nine years, but he was still the bloody earl.

"No, I will not do that," Maureen said. "Marcus, you have only been back in London for two days. We had no notion of when you would return. As Clarissa says, we have been living on our own, and doing quite well, I might add, despite this recent debacle. I already scheduled a meeting with this person because it was up to me to handle matters." She took a few steps down the corridor, as if that settled everything. "Now then, it would make the situation much better if you would join us in the meeting, but we do not require your permission."

He eyed his aunt, who had, for all intents and purposes, just laid him out. "Who is this person, the one who can solve this problem?"

"Vivian March. The Paragon."

The name had sounded vaguely familiar, but Marcus couldn't place it. Vivian March. Well, she would be here soon enough and he could meet her then. His aunt had assured him that this woman, who was evidently referred to as The Paragon, would be able to divert attention from the scandal, effectively making it disappear, before it did much damage. But in order for that to happen, she would have to agree to align herself with them, which would require a certain amount of decorum from him.

Marcus had never been particularly good at playing society's games. It was one of the reasons he'd left London to begin with. He much preferred the wilds of Africa and India to the well-polished, pretentious behavior he found here. At least in the wild, animals acted in the interests of survival. People did not adhere to such courtesies.

But he'd agreed, for this evening, to mind his manners, and to meet with this woman to see if she could assist his sister. So it was that he and Clarissa and their Aunt Maureen sat silently waiting for this Paragon to appear. At precisely seven, the butler opened the door and announced her.

"Miss Vivian March."

The woman entered the room covered in a burgundy velvet cloak. She withdrew the hood and then slid out of the contraption, allowing the butler to remove it. She wasn't overly tall and had generous curves that filled her pale pink satin ball gown nicely without being too revealing. Chocolate brown curls were expertly piled on her head in an intricate coiffure. Long black satin gloves covered her hands and slid all the way up to just past her elbows. She was the picture of English modesty.

"Thank you so much for coming, Miss March," Aunt Maureen said, coming forward to greet the woman.

Vivian March tilted her head, and he finally saw her entire face. His gut knotted as a jolt of recognition struck him. *Now* he knew why her name sounded familiar. He knew her. Or at least, he had known her, had met her. Briefly.

He stepped forward to make his own greeting. Her eyes met his. She didn't even flinch. In fact, she showed no sign at all that she recognized him. But he knew one thing for certain about Miss Vivian March.

She was no paragon.

"My Lord, it is my understanding you have recently returned from traveling abroad," she said. Her voice was rich and sultry, full of seductive promise.

"I have. And it would seem my family is in a bit of turmoil. I was told you might be of some assistance."

She inclined her head, then turned to Maureen before she spoke. "Perhaps we should sit and you can tell me more about the situation."

"Yes, of course," Aunt Maureen said. She rang for the tea tray with cakes and they all sat in the parlor. "Please do sit, Miss March, and thank you again for coming on such short notice."

Miss March sat in a high-backed chair, but if it was

possible, sat even straighter than the wood back. Her gloved hands rested on her lap and a pleasant smile played at her lips.

Clarissa had yet to utter a word. Instead, she sat staring at her hands as they knotted the fabric of her skirt. Perhaps she was still angry with him for his behavior earlier today.

Marcus leaned against the mantel and watched the women sugar and stir their tea. How could Miss March not recognize him? He knew for certain it was she, though now ten years older. Womanhood had softened and rounded her figure to a voluptuousness he could scarcely look away from.

After she had taken a sip of her tea, she glanced first at Aunt Maureen, then at Clarissa. "Now, what seems to be the problem?"

"Nothing," Clarissa said. She set her teacup down and offered a feigned smile. "I had a conversation with a gentleman. That is all that happened. It is unclear to me why this has to be such an ordeal."

"Yes, well, what actually happens and what *might* have happened are not always perceived differently," Miss March said. "So you had a conversation with a gentleman. Is he truly a gentleman, or is that simply his species? Also, was this conversation held in private or in a public location?"

He half expected the woman to draw out a notebook and begin making notes, but she simply waited for Clarissa to answer. When there was a long pause, Miss March spoke again, this time looking directly at him. "Perhaps the young lady would feel more comfortable if she and I spoke alone."

He had lost count as to how many times he'd been dismissed today by the women in this house. Perhaps he wasn't as prepared to handle this sort of situation the way

Charles would have been, but damnation, he'd only just returned to London. They might not want him to be the head of the family, and they might not believe him to be competent, but he wasn't going anywhere.

Marcus shoved off the mantel and walked toward Miss March. "*This* is a family affair. And whether or not the women in my family approve or not, I am part of this family. You were called here to help us. If my sister refuses to cooperate, then I'll tell you what happened. The chit was seen talking to the owner of a gaming establishment."

Miss March nodded, and while she looked at him while he spoke, her body was still angled toward where Maureen and Clarissa sat.

He turned to his sister. "Were you sitting in the carriage, or standing on the street?"

"On the street," she said, her eyes locked on tea tray in front of her.

Miss March patted Clarissa's knee. She was quiet for a few moments, then took another sip of her tea. "Yes, well, I can see why we have a potential problem. Do you know, perhaps, who saw you? That is, who brought this matter to your attention?" she asked Clarissa.

"Lady Jessup informed me at a card party yesterday," Aunt Maureen said.

"Well, I can only guess it was her husband who saw you then, Clarissa. Lord Jessup is a horrific gambler and an even worse gossip. Chances are that other people know now. So it would seem that you definitely have a potentially damaging situation on your hands." She came to her feet.

Aunt Maureen stood as well. "Will you help us?"

"I shall consider it this evening and will be in touch

tomorrow morning." She straightened her gloves and patted her hair.

"Is that all?" Marcus asked, not quite certain what he'd been expecting. But a woman who came, sipped tea, confirmed that yes indeed, they were in trouble, then fled, was not precisely the big solution he'd been waiting for.

"I must consider the situation," she said.

"I'll walk you out," he said.

"That truly won't be necessary." Miss March made her way to the door.

Marcus followed her regardless of her dismissive tone. He took her cloak from the butler. "I'm offended that you would pretend not to remember me." He held the cloak away from her, forcing her to turn and look in his direction.

She looked up at him, her warm brown eyes meeting his gaze. "I beg your pardon?" she said, her voice full of innocence.

So it was a game she intended to play. Well, a game he would give her.

He draped the cloak over her shoulders, then bent to her ear. "Just remember that I know the truth. I know you are not the paragon people believe you to be." There was a sharp intake of her breath. "Until tomorrow, Miss March."

Chapter Two

Who did he think he was? Vivian wondered as she settled herself in the carriage seat.

Of course she remembered him. Heavens, she could never forget Marcus Kincaid, and now he was back. Not only back in London, but back in her life, it would seem.

She shivered as she remembered his warm breath across her neck and shoulder as he'd wrapped her in her cloak. She remembered much more. His kiss. His embrace. That night had changed the course of her life forever. The night that Frederick had broken her heart and she realized she had become a fallen woman. She had worked tirelessly the past ten years to forget that evening, but it seemed that some mistakes could not be left behind.

Marcus Kincaid hadn't changed, except that he'd clearly become more of a man. His hair was longer, and the hint of a beard had shaded his cheeks and chin. His lovely blue eyes were as pretty as she remembered, though they held a bit of worldliness now. He was larger too, broader, and more masculine than he'd been a decade before.

And he'd thought to threaten her. She would never have agreed to the meeting had she known he'd returned.

Nevertheless, she was a woman of virtue now and nothing would change that, and she'd be damned if she allowed him to destroy all she'd worked for. He had certainly put her in a predicament. She might not have been interested in aligning herself with Lord Ashford and the Kincaid family, but he'd given her no choice in the matter. She wasn't certain he'd been making a threat, but he did know things about her no one else knew. So she *would* be aligning herself with the Kincaid family, after all. Therefore, the first thing she needed was a plan to make Clarissa's scandal disappear, and then a second plan to make certain Vivian didn't have to spend more time with Lord Ashford than was absolutely necessary.

Instead of attending the soiree she had dressed for, she instructed her driver to return her to her townhouse. She had scarcely entered the front door when her Aunt Rose called to her from the blue parlor. The last time she'd seen Marcus Kincaid, she'd come home distraught. That night she'd fallen apart in front of both of her aunts. It had been nearly six years since Aunt Lillian had passed. So much had changed since then. Primarily, Vivian had changed. Despite the way she felt at the moment, she didn't have the luxury to fall apart. She prided herself on maintaining control at all times. Yet, one conversation with Marcus Kincaid and she felt all heated and flustered.

"Vivian, why are you home so early?" Aunt Rose asked.

Vivian took a sobering breath and stepped into the parlor. She found her aunt sitting at her writing table, stacking her playing cards into a complex tower.

"Would you allow me to retreat to my room if I simply complained of a headache?" Vivian asked.

Aunt Rose looked at her above her spectacles as if considering the offer. "No. Now, spill it." She removed her glasses and turned to face her niece. "Tell me what has happened with the Ashford family."

Vivian peeled off her gloves, then waved one of them dismissively. "The typical trouble a young woman would find herself in. Naturally, there's a man involved, though I'll admit she has some panache." Vivian took a seat on the gold upholstered settee. "I shall have to have a private conversation with her at some point to get the full truth of the situation, but it would seem she had some manner of rendezvous with the owner of a gaming hell."

"Brazen. Or foolish," Rose said.

"Indeed."

"But that is not what troubles you."

"No, I don't suppose it is." Vivian steeled herself before speaking. There was no need to panic. She had prepared for ten years for his return, knowing full well that eventually he would and she would see him. But it wasn't his return that was troublesome. It was the thought that if he could return, then so could Frederick, and she did not think there would ever be enough time to prepare her for that reunion. For now, though, she merely had to manage the man she'd kissed by accident.

"Marcus Kincaid is back. He has taken his place as the new earl."

Rose nodded gravely. "A little late. His brother was buried months ago, was he not?"

"Yes. The family was unable to reach Marcus because of the nature of his travels."

"His return bothers you." Rose pulled off her spectacles and wiped them methodically on her sleeve.

"And you think it should not?" When Rose nodded, Vivian continued. "Aunt, I kissed him, if you recall. Quite brazenly. All the while fully believing him to be another man."

Rose waved her spectacles in front of her, then replaced them on her nose. "Yes, but it has been years. I should think he would have forgotten, especially now that he is so worldly. Did he even remember you?"

Vivian eyed her aunt looking for signs of jesting, but found none. "He does remember. He didn't say anything specifically about the kiss. Instead, he tossed out a remark about knowing that I'm not the paragon people believe me to be. He remembered me."

"Well, you've never cared for that ridiculous nickname," Rose said.

She did hate the moniker, but without it all her work would be for naught. People trusted her. They believed her to be the very pinnacle of propriety, and in that belief lay all of her power, all of her ability to manipulate the truth and hide one scandal after another. Were it not for her, London society would be the tenth circle in Dante's *Divine Comedy*. So she might not prefer the name she'd been given, but it was necessary for the service she provided. "Quite true. Still, it is somewhat embarrassing to see him again after all these years."

"For something you did ten years ago? Pish-posh, every woman is allowed one indiscretion. He was yours. You are older and wiser now. There is no need to spend another moment thinking about a little kiss."

True, but it had been a kiss to end all kisses, despite the fact that she'd thought she'd been kissing someone else. Still, the one moment she'd shared with Marcus Kincaid had most assuredly been memorable—and not simply because it was the beginning of the worst night of her life.

She had never told her aunts the full truth of the situation. They'd known she'd kissed Marcus by mistake and that Frederick had left her. But she'd kept her affair with Frederick a secret. Of course she'd waited to see if she'd been carrying Frederick's child, knowing she might have to tell them what had happened, but that had never come to pass. She knew her aunts would have loved her regardless of the situation, but the shame still ate at her, so she'd kept the full truth to herself. And that affair, if discovered, could simply ruin her.

"I suppose I shouldn't have pretended to not remember him. Perhaps I wounded his pride and that was why he threatened me," Vivian said.

"Oh yes, men do not manage such injuries well. So what will you do?"

"I have no choice. I will take on Miss Kincaid's scandal and clear her path. Hopefully she'll be married by the end of the Season and no one will be the wiser."

. . .

Vivian was shown into the very same parlor where she'd met the Kincaid family the night before. It was early afternoon and she'd carefully drafted a plan to douse this scandal before too much damage was caused. It would take their entire family, though, so she'd need everyone's cooperation.

A moment later the two women, Maureen and Clarissa, entered the room.

"Is Lord Ashford not in?" Vivian asked. She immediately chided herself for sounding disappointed that she would not see him. What did it matter if she saw him or not? Who cared if she'd stayed up half the evening preparing a speech to give him on why it was important for his sister's sake that no one know the truth about the incident they'd shared several years before?

"He is here," Clarissa said with an unladylike roll of her eyes. "He's merely taking his own leisurely time in coming downstairs."

"Clarissa," Maureen chided. "Mind yourself."

Clarissa nodded. "My apologies."

"It is of no matter to me," Vivian said. "I suspect it is quite difficult to welcome a brother who has been gone for so much of your life. He is but a stranger to you, is he not?" It was none of her business to pry, but she was here to help the family, and that gave her some privilege to their private information.

"Precisely. I do not know him." Clarissa sat on the settee near Vivian. "And he does not know me."

"Well, that will change if we are to make this little problem of yours disappear." Vivian patted the girl's hand. "Now then, why don't we discuss more of what occurred that day with the man outside of the gaming hell, and then I shall detail my plan."

"You are taking the job, as it were?" a masculine voice asked from the doorway.

She looked up to see Lord Ashford leaning against the

doorjamb. He cut a fine figure standing there with a casual air about him. His too-long hair should make him appear unkempt and slovenly, but instead it gave him an air of rebellion and danger that only increased his attractiveness. His black jacket hugged his broad shoulders nicely, and Vivian immediately found it vastly annoying that she had noticed any of that.

"My lord," she said curtly. He raised his eyebrows and she realized she had not answered his question. "Yes—that is, yes, I shall be assisting your family in this situation."

He nodded, but made no move to enter the room.

She turned her attention away from him and forced herself to look at Clarissa. "I will need more details about what specifically you were doing at that gaming establishment. It is not in a neighborhood where ladies tend to venture. What were you doing there, really?"

Clarissa shrugged. "I had important matters to discuss with Mr. Rodale."

"You sought him out?" Vivian asked.

"I did. "

"Rodale?" Marcus asked. "As in Justin Rodale?"

"Yes," Clarissa said.

"You know him?" Vivian asked Marcus.

"I do. We went to Cambridge together. We were mates. He had been to the house. Clarissa would have met him, though that would have been years ago. I did not realize he owned a gambling establishment," Marcus said, then shrugged. "But I have been out of the country for a while."

"What matters could you possibly have to discuss with the owner of a gaming hell?" Maureen asked, clearly exasperated, as if this were a matter they'd been over before.

Vivian watched Clarissa's mouth work as she waged an internal war on what to say. The girl was not ready to talk, but what went on in that meeting was vital information if Vivian was to keep her reputation intact.

"Clarissa, I understand your reluctance to speak, but it really is imperative that I have all the details. I can assure you, you have my pledge that I shall guard your secret as closely as I would one of my own." It was what she told all of her clients, and though they never bothered to consider whether she actually had any secrets, she meant what she said. Their secrets were all she had to hide her own private scandal.

Clarissa nodded. "I went to see Mr. Rodale about a friend's debts. I wanted to pay them."

"Clarissa, what money do you have to pay for such a thing?" Aunt Maureen asked.

Clarissa shrugged and gave a half smile. "How many hair ribbons does a woman need? I've put money aside for a while on the off chance I would need some."

"Who is this friend?" Vivian asked.

"George Wilbanks. He has been a friend for many years."

"She is sweet on the boy," Aunt Maureen said.

Vivian saw no reason to comment. Inwardly, she cringed for Clarissa, wanting to warn her about setting her cap for a man who would allow a woman to pay his gambling debts, but that was for another day. "And did you pay his debts?" she asked.

Clarissa sat straighter, inspected her fingernails, then folded her hands in her lap. "I did not. Mr. Rodale was quite difficult—boorish, if you ask me—about the entire matter. He didn't want to talk to me at all. He kept trying to send me on my way, but I was rather insistent. It was not an overly long conversation, and ultimately I left unable to settle the debts. He lied and told me George did not have any debts. That he was, in fact, a frequent guest at the establishment, but that he had had a run of good luck lately and did not have any outstanding debts."

Vivian saw something flicker in Clarissa's blue eyes, eyes very similar to her brother's. It seemed as though the girl were angry. "Why is it that you believe him to be lying to you?"

"He was clearly lying. George specifically told me it was that hell where he had lost such a large sum. If the debt is paid, why does it matter from where the funds come?" Clarissa frowned, then shook her head. "I tried to give George the money directly to pay off the debt, but he refused, which is why I went to see Mr. Rodale myself. I thought since he and Marcus had been friends, he might remember me and we would be able to work out an agreement."

Vivian watched a moment longer, knowing that Mr. Rodale would probably have a different story to tell, but she would reserve judgment on whether or not she would need to pay him a visit as well. "Well, that certainly clarifies matters for me. So your virtue remains intact. You merely had a conversation in an inappropriate place, but with a man who could be considered a friend of the family," Vivian said. "Now, before I go into detail as to how we will handle this situation, I need you all to agree that you will stand by Clarissa no matter what happens. We must present a united front."

"You sound like an army general." Marcus shoved off the door and finally stepped into the room. He made his way to a chair and sat, extending his long legs out in front of him. Black trousers encased his legs, but Vivian couldn't help wondering if they'd be as lean and muscular as she suspected they were.

What had come over her? She never imagined such impure thoughts about a gentleman. Once she'd settled herself on being a spinster, she rarely considered men at all. Clearly, Marcus was a constant reminder of her past. Of her poor choices and her weak nature.

"Do you have other family members we can call upon?" Vivian asked.

"Yes, we have cousins," Clarissa said.

"Cousins?" Marcus asked.

"Lena and her husband, Henry. Certainly you must remember them?" Clarissa asked.

Marcus nodded, but did not respond to his sister's anger. "Of course."

"Clarissa, you mustn't speak to your brother with such anger." This was the primary problem with most people, Vivian recognized. They simply were too careless with their own emotions. She knew one could control one's feelings; she'd been doing it for a decade. It had taken considerable practice, but she'd mastered it all the same. "You can certainly feel it, you have every right, but that is a private matter that you and he must deal with here in your home. Out there, in the midst of others in London, it is imperative that everyone believe you are a loving and supportive family."

Marcus watched Vivian as she instructed his sister. As he

surveyed her motions, her voice faded to the background. Her hands moved as she spoke and her facial expressions revealed her concern and her seriousness about the situation. Vivian March was full of heat and intensity. Perhaps to some she might simply appear concerned, but he could see the truth simmering behind her eyes—she was full of passion. And those eyes were now looking directly at him, expectantly.

"Did you hear me, Lord Ashford?" she asked. One delicate eyebrow rose slowly. Seductively, even.

"I'm afraid I did not," he said. He gave her what he knew to be his most charming smile.

She faltered, though only slightly. "A dinner party, at my home tomorrow. To reintroduce you to society as the new earl. Only a handful of families will be invited. The more exclusive, the better."

"If you think that will work, we shall be there," he said.

"What do you mean, *if* I think it will work?" she asked, clearly incensed.

The butler stepped into the room. "Lady Atkins is here for your shopping trip, Lady Clarissa."

Clarissa shot to her feet. "Yes, I had nearly forgotten that was today. I am to help her select some new dresses."

Aunt Maureen also stood. "And I am to chaperone." She eyed Vivian. "If we need to reschedule, though, we can. A situation this delicate is obviously more important than shopping."

"No," Vivian said with a nod and a wave of her hand. "It will actually be good for Clarissa to be seen out, doing normal activities. Perhaps you should buy a new dress or two."

"As many as you need," Marcus said when he realized Maureen was watching him keenly. Evidently, he wasn't allowed to handle potential scandals, but he was expected to dole out money when it was needed to purchase new party dresses. Clarissa did her best to keep her gaze off him. He wasn't certain if she was simply still punishing him for being gone so long or if she genuinely didn't care what he had to say.

The two other women nodded and left the room, leaving him alone with Vivian March. At least with her he didn't feel so out of his element, not as he did with the women in his family.

Vivian whipped around to face him. "I do not take kindly to your sarcasm."

He almost laughed. Perhaps he was not nearly as charming with women as he'd once thought. He leveled his gaze on Vivian. "Sarcasm. To what are you referring?"

"Your cutting remark about my plan. You might not believe I know what I'm doing, but I have been assisting families with these types of situations for many years while you've been off traipsing across heaven knows where."

"Precisely how many families are we talking about? Seems to me that if you are known as the woman to go to whenever there is a scandal, then once you aligned yourself with someone, everyone would know that there was, in fact, a scandal." He shrugged. "Counterproductive, wouldn't you agree?"

"No, I would not agree," she said tartly. "I said I have worked with many families, but not so many that people would take notice. Furthermore, what I do is not commonly known. I take my clients' lives quite seriously and discretion is of utmost importance to me."

Her eyes flared with intensity and her cheeks flushed.

Discretion could be a good thing when one was behaving badly.

He couldn't help wondering, if pushed, how wickedly Miss March could behave.

Chapter Three

Marcus grinned at her. "You are lovely when you get angry, do you know that?"

"Do not change the subject. Why do you think my plan is faulty?" she demanded.

"I don't think people are foolish enough to ignore her indiscretion simply because I have returned to England." He shrugged. "That is not interesting news."

"Oh, but that is where you're wrong. Your return is most assuredly news." She smiled, a genuine smile that lit her eyes and exposed large dimples in each cheek. "The travel-weary brother has returned to take the helm of the family. You have a younger sister to marry off, and you have many adventures of which you can speak. You have been to many exotic lands, have you not?"

"I have been to a great many places," he said with a nod. She took these matters quite seriously and for some odd reason he found that vastly attractive. Of course, he took his family seriously, too. She was right. He was at the helm, as it were, and whether his sister liked it or not, she was his responsibility now. He did need to see her married, and after what she'd said in this very room earlier, she was content to marry a fool who had a gambling problem. She obviously needed assistance selecting a better choice in a husband, and if Vivian March could provide that he would gladly pay her.

"How is it that we pay you for your services?"

She waved a gloved hand. "I am a very wealthy woman, Lord Ashford, and therefore I do not accept monetary payment. The only thing I ask of my families is that they provide me a favor when I call upon them to do so."

A barter system built on favors. Fascinating. "Precisely how many families here in London owe you favors, Miss March?"

She smiled coyly. "It would be indiscreet of me to answer. Suffice it to say, I am well connected and have a great many people to call upon should I need something."

"Interesting," he said. She was becoming more and more fascinating by the moment.

"Consider that we might have use of one such favor for this situation with your sister," she said.

"I wasn't arguing. It's clever, and potentially makes you quite powerful, but then again, you are the Paragon, are you not?"

"The moniker is unnecessary," she said.

"You do not care for it?"

"It was not a name I came up with, if that's what you're asking." She picked a piece of lint off her skirts, then smoothed a nonexistent wrinkle from them. "Now then, at the dinner party, you must come prepared to discuss your many adventures. It will be all people will want to hear."

"I doubt people will be that intrigued. I have led tours for members of some of these very families. Certainly, they will have come back with their own tales," he said.

"You, my lord, have been out of polite society long enough to forget how they are. That is precisely why they will want to hear your version. They'll want to know all the gossip about the other families." She came to her feet. "My plan will work. You must trust me."

He stood too. "I'm not so certain I can do that, Miss March." He took several steps toward her.

She stood in the middle of the room, hand to throat, staring back at him. Staring precisely at his chest. He crossed his arms over said chest and smiled at her. Her cheekbones raised high, her eyebrows arched gracefully, outlining her warm brown eyes with thick, dark lashes. Her mouth, pink and almost too full, formed a small *O*. A blush tinted her cheeks and the part of her neck still visible around her hand. Lovely brown hair, swept up from her face, revealed a clear view of her milky complexion. Not one blemish marred her skin. Except for the tiny lines curving from her lips and the ones fanning out from her eyes, her skin was as lovely as any woman ten years her junior.

He rather liked the lines; they meant she smiled a lot, but the hint of a line above her brow meant she also frowned. He appreciated both sentiments. Most people only appreciated a pretty smile, just as most of the English enjoyed only sweet foods. But in all his travels, he'd come to appreciate the mixture of different flavors. Sweet blended with fiery spice suited his palate quite nicely.

He took another step toward her, looking straight in her

face. "Miss March, you are a most handsome woman. Might I be so bold as to inquire your age?"

Her breath caught audibly. She frowned. "Lord Ashford, that is certainly none of your concern. I must request you refrain from making such remarks to me. I am far too old to play your parlor games."

"I was playing no game. I meant precisely what I said. I'll admit it was not very gentlemanly to inquire about your age, but I do believe you were not in your first Season when we met in that garden, were you?" He didn't wait for her response. "I grant you, I was impossibly rude to inquire, but I am at a loss as to deciphering your precise age."

She opened her mouth then promptly shut it.

He knew that by London standards he was behaving outrageously, but flirting with Miss Vivian March proved most entertaining. Not to mention a temptation he simply couldn't resist.

"I prefer women of a certain age," he said. "I find them refreshingly honest. Intelligent, with minds of their own." He took another step, closing the distance between them. "And remarkably passionate." His remark did little more than keep her locked in her current position, though her eyes widened slightly. He slid one finger down her arm. "But with your lovely skin, I would guess you are not a day older than seven and twenty."

She snorted uncharacteristically. "I am four and thirty." She raised her eyebrows, then blew out a breath. "You goaded me into admitting that, sir. I will not be so foolish the next time." She swallowed visibly. "Now, would you be so kind as to tell me why you will be unable to trust me in this endeavor with your sister? If you cannot trust me, my lord, this plan to salvage her reputation will never succeed."

"Ah, yes, why I don't trust you. Well, you are still pretending not to remember me, not to know me. But I know you remember."

She shook her head vehemently.

"Indeed. Well, then allow me to refresh your memory." With one hand he tilted her chin so he could have perfect access to her mouth. He pressed his mouth to hers.

She gasped, her hands fisted on his chest, but he continued to kiss her. Softer than he remembered, perhaps even fuller, Vivian's lips were heaven to move across. He slid his tongue over her bottom lip and her body tensed. He moved his tongue into her mouth and began his slow seduction.

Coaxing her with his lips and tongue, he moved across her mouth, urging her to participate.

Her body felt deliciously curvaceous against his. He deepened the kiss, finally earning a response from her. Her arms wrapped around his neck, her fingers spreading into his hair. Her tongue met his, stroke for stroke, and he groaned with his need for her. He could kiss her forever. But that would have to wait for another day.

He ended the kiss, pulling back from her. She stood, clutched in his arms, eyes closed and lips parted, her breath labored. In that moment, he had never seen a more alluring, more seductive woman. He wagered he would regret it later, but he stepped away from her.

"Are you going to tell me you don't remember me?"

Her eyes shot open.

"I realize it has been a long while and the last time we kissed you were the one to instigate it, but certainly you remember."

She exhaled slowly, tugged on her jacket, and tilted up

her chin. "Lord Ashford, you are a cad."

"Perhaps."

"What transpired between us happened very long ago. It is not something I remember with fondness. It was a mistake, as I told you then. Not my worst mistake, but certainly a close second."

So she had made other mistakes. That was something worth investigating.

"Now then, what will it take to make you forget that little piece of my personal history?" she asked.

He smiled. "Ah, yes, another favor. I believe I shall consider that. I'll let you know at a later date the price for my silence."

A tic in her jaw betrayed her frustration, but she nodded all the same. "Very well. At the dinner party, I expect you and your family to be prompt. You all have a good impression to make."

He bowed slightly. "We shall be at your service."

"That, I highly doubt. Good day, Lord Ashford." She turned on her heel and left.

Vivian finally exhaled as the carriage door closed. The rig rolled down the street, leaving the Ashford townhouse to make the short distance to her own. Good heavens. She pulled at the lace edging her bodice. She wanted to turn her mind to something other than that searing kiss, but it consumed her thoughts. And how could it not? It had been delicious. She released a slow breath. There was no other way to consider it. She had thought the kiss they'd shared ten years ago had been potent. Perhaps it had been so long she'd forgotten. She doubted it, though. This one seemed even more passionate, more intense, more intimate. Even now, her skin still tingled. Her fingers went to her mouth.

She shook herself. She was not in the business of receiving kisses, let alone enjoyable ones. He had kissed her only to knock her off kilter, and she recognized that.

Marcus Kincaid was a man who preferred to be in charge and the women in his family had made a mess while he'd been away. Flirting with her gave him the upper hand. It was harmless, she reminded herself. Once Clarissa's scandal was contained, he would leave Vivian alone.

The carriage arrived at her house and she stepped onto the sidewalk. Across the street, another carriage was parked, one that looked faintly familiar. She eyed the worn crest on the door, but the paint had faded so much that she couldn't recognize much of it. In the tiny window a curtain pulled back and someone looked out at her. Then the curtain shut and the carriage rolled away.

Someone was watching her.

• • •

Clarissa stepped into the study, but left the door ajar. "You wanted to see me?"

"Yes. I received notice from Miss March about the dinner party this evening. She wanted to inform us ahead of time that she had invited Justin Rodale and that he accepted," Marcus said.

"She what?" Clarissa asked, her arms crossed over her chest. He half expected her to stamp her foot. In that moment he remembered her as she'd been when he'd left ten years before. She'd been but a girl then, pretty, with bouncing curls and always a passel of dolls clutched in her arms. He'd missed her growing up into the woman that stood before him. "Why the devil would she do such a thing?"

It was on his tongue to chide her for cursing, but if he constantly corrected her, she'd never again trust him. It was much like approaching an animal in the wild—you had to be still and calm and then they would eventually get used to your presence. "You said yourself you went to speak to him directly, to appeal to him personally because he and I had once been friends. This is to keep up appearances about that story. Justin and I haven't seen each other since Cambridge, but we were mates." In truth, he hadn't yet decided how he felt about Justin being there. But he honestly wasn't looking forward to much about tonight, mingling with people he hadn't seen in years and others that he hadn't yet met. The only thing he was looking forward to was seeing Miss March again.

Clarissa shook her head. "It still seems completely unnecessary, but I suppose if he's going to be there, it's best that she wouldn't agree to invite George."

According to Aunt Maureen, Clarissa had set her cap for this Wilbanks fellow, but at this point Marcus was uncertain if it was a good match. The inconsistency in the man's story and what had happened with Justin made Marcus question whether the man had any interest in marrying his sister in the first place. Yet he seemed to be keeping her around—as an alternate, perhaps. It was enough to make Marcus want to call on the man, but he hadn't been in town long enough to know the full story. Perhaps Justin could shed some light on the situation tonight if they had a quiet moment to speak.

"We shall make the best of it," Marcus said.

"I still do not understand why we have to carry on so. Is it truly such an ordeal for me to have had a conversation with a man on the street?" Clarissa asked.

"You know it is."

"Well, it shouldn't be. There is nothing at all inappropriate in having a conversation with someone. People shouldn't be so antiquated."

"Rather forward thinking of you," he said. "Still, you had no business being in that part of town." Marcus softened his tone. "You should have asked for help."

"From whom?" Clarissa's eyebrows rose. "*You* weren't here."

He opened his mouth to say something, to give her an explanation for his absence, but voices in the corridor saved him before he could.

"Where is that world-traveling cousin of mine?" Marcus heard Lena's teasing voice in the entryway of the main hall.

"Lena," Clarissa said softly. She brightened and turned on her heel, leaving the study.

Marcus rounded the door and caught sight of the tall redhead smiling brightly at his sister.

"Clarissa, love, you look so pretty this morning," Lena said. "And Marcus," she said as she walked toward him, arms open. "My goodness, it's been so long and you are a full-grown man." She held him out so she could see all of him. "And quite a handsome one, too."

Her husband, Henry Covington, Viscount Glenfield, entered the door wiping raindrops from his coat. "It grows nastier out there every minute. We couldn't have left at a better time, Lena, dear. Good day to you, Marcus old boy."

Henry's jovial tone bellowed down the hall.

Marcus embraced Lena and kissed her cheek. "I have been a man for quite a while, Lena, but thank you."

"I have missed you, cousin," she said. She held him tightly and he felt the love radiate from her. He swallowed hard. It was more difficult to hold the world at arm's length being this close to his family. But he'd be a liar if he said he hadn't missed them, too. All of them. He stepped away from her and reached for Henry's hand for a few quick shakes. "And you as well, Henry. I hope you're ready for tonight's festivities."

"We shall do anything to help," Lena said. She grabbed Clarissa's hand. "You should have written to me sooner."

Clarissa shook her head. "It is nothing. Truly."

"Miss March has assured us this little dinner party will assist in diverting everyone's attention," Marcus said.

Lena's expression lit her eyes. "Miss March? Vivian March? How delightful."

"You know Miss March?" Marcus asked.

"Indeed. A finer woman you couldn't find if you searched all of London," Lena said. "It promises to be a most entertaining evening."

Chapter Four

Vivian washed her face with the tepid water from the pitcher and changed into a lovely dress the color of rich sable. Based on Vivian's instructions, her maid pulled her hair into a loose coiffure so that soft curls framed her face. Aunt Lillian had always said it looked pretty like this, simple and feminine. But it did beg the question, for whom did Vivian need to look pretty?

Marcus Kincaid's handsome face flashed into her mind. With his unfashionably long hair and a face that always looked a little in need of a shave, he was ridiculously handsome. She rolled her eyes. And his handsomeness, ridiculous or not, had absolutely no relevance to her life.

She reached up to fiddle with her hair and the metal pins pinched as she tightened them. She had been disciplined for far too long to allow one man to tempt her into ignoring everything she'd worked so hard for. Yet, since his kiss the day before, she'd been walking around much like a lost goose, so distracted was she.

And she had actually not required him to remind her of their original kiss. In the last ten years there had been many nights that she'd gone to sleep replaying every second of the blasted thing. Now she had another by which to compare. They were different in many ways. Their fist kiss had been a surprise. She'd kissed him and he'd merely accepted what she'd given, but it had been the kiss of a young man. This time, though, it had been controlled, deliberate, and full of simmering heat. But the kisses had had one very disturbing thing in common—her damned reaction. She sighed.

"Begging your pardon, ma'am, am I doing something wrong?" her maid asked.

"No, sorry, I'm merely distracted." She caught a glimpse of herself in the mirror. "I think that will be all for tonight. Thank you." The girl stepped out and Vivian stared at herself. Her dress was lovely and modestly cut so as to not reveal too much of her ample curves. Admittedly, her hair did look pretty, but what did it truly matter? She was of an age that made it less important to be attractive. She was quite certain that she was almost old enough to start wearing stuffed birds in her hat plumage. Even Marcus had inquired as to her age and she'd foolishly told him—as if it were any of his concern.

For whatever reason, she seemed to do and say plenty around Marcus that went against her better judgment. She would have to be vigilant and focused. Tonight was about introducing him as the earl, so she couldn't very well ignore him, but she needed to keep as many people around them as possible. It was imperative that she not be alone with the man lest she make any other foolish mistakes.

Vivian took a deep breath and stepped into the parlor that lay adjacent to her dining room. Already many of her guests had arrived and she smiled broadly to welcome them. Her aunt sat in her favorite chair with her tabby curled up behind her. Two of Rose's matronly friends sat near her and they visited quietly. A man she did not know stood near the hearth, a glass in his hand. He nodded to her and she smiled in return. That must be Mr. Rodale. She stepped toward him. He was handsome in an almost wild sort of way, with hair as black as ink and eyes equally as dark. His complexion spoke of perhaps a French or other European heritage; he wasn't nearly as pale as most Englishmen. His smile was genuine, though, as he walked to meet her.

"Miss March, I presume," he said.

"Indeed, and I suppose you are Mr. Rodale. So very kind of you to join us this evening," she said. Her invitation to him had not been as explicit as it could have been. She'd opted to try and be coy and then proceed with additional details if the moment called for it. But she'd merely invited him to welcome his old friend, Marcus Kincaid, as he made his first public appearance as the Earl of Ashford.

"Thank you for inviting me," he said.

"Of course. Any friend of Lord Ashford's is a friend of mine," she said.

"Is that so?" a decidedly male voice asked from behind her.

Her blood warmed at his presence, which annoyed her more than a little. "My lord," she said as she turned to face him. Had she not been careful, her breath would have caught at the sight of him. He was dashing. More than dashing in a black tailored suit that only served to enhance his broad shoulders and showcase his long legs. Tonight, he was clean-shaven, and the absence of even a hint of whiskers only served to bring attention to his firm jaw and perfectly curved lips. There was simply no reason for a man to be that attractive. But it wasn't merely his handsomeness. Mr. Rodale was just as dashing, perhaps even more so, with his dark, exotic features, yet she certainly wasn't reacting to him the way she did to Marcus.

"Miss March, you look lovely," he said. His blue eyes trailed the length of her, and settled back on her face. He could not have warmed her more had he inspected her with his hands. She felt her cheeks flame and she swallowed hard.

"Justin, good of you to join us. It's been a while," he said to Mr. Rodale. They exchanged handshakes.

"It has been. Too long," Justin said. "Though I admit I was surprised to be included on the guest list."

Marcus eyed Vivian. "I may be the earl now, but the thought of being surrounded by stodgy aristocrats, exclusively, was enough to give me hives."

"You are a stodgy aristocrat, are you not?" Justin asked.

"Aristocrat, perhaps, but stodgy? Never," Marcus said with a grin.

"I am most eager to hear of your adventures," Justin said. "I have no doubt you have many stories you could share." He leaned closer to them. "Primarily the humorous ones about English buffoons making asses of themselves." His dark eyes fell on Vivian. "My apologies, Miss March, it is not often that I am invited to attend polite society. Perhaps now we know why."

"No need for the apology, sir. It is not the first time I've heard a curse, and will not likely be the last." She nodded to the men. "If you'll both excuse me, I have other guests I need to welcome."

She made her way over to Clarissa and the couple standing behind her. She knew Marcus and Clarissa's cousin, Lena, from school, but it had been a long while since she'd spoken to her, though they had seen one another on occasion at balls over the last several years.

"I do not understand why he had to be invited," Clarissa said quietly when Vivian reached her side.

"He's charming, and a friend of your brother's. Remember, that is why you were speaking with him. Besides, perhaps this will give you another opportunity to discuss your friend's debts. Though you would obviously want to be quite discreet." She watched Clarissa's eyes soften, and Vivian knew she had said the right thing to convince the girl of the plan. She squeezed her arm encouragingly. "All will be well, Clarissa. You don't need to spend the entire evening with him. We merely want to establish you as family friends. So do try to be pleasant."

Clarissa nodded. "I don't suppose you took my suggestion to invite George?" she asked, her eyes scanning the room.

"I did not. We already had a full table, and I suspect you see enough of him at your regular parties. Tonight we have the opportunity to meet some new people. You will have a lovely time, I promise. Now let me say hello to your cousins."

"Vivian," Lena said, as Vivian guided Clarissa over to the other woman.

Vivian smiled at the tall, slender redhead. "Lena, how wonderful it is to see you. Until yesterday, I did not realize you were a cousin to the Kincaids. How lovely of you to join us this evening."

They embraced, and the smooth silkiness of Lena's dress against Vivian's hand reminded her of her own dress's sensible style. Lena's rich, plum-colored dress fit her perfectly and flounced in all the latest fashion, with its square neckline and ruffled skirt. The satin beautifully complimented her alabaster skin.

There was a time when Vivian had dressed in the height of fashion. She could certainly afford it. But in the last several years she'd instructed her *modiste* to cut her dresses along more modest lines. She was a confirmed spinster. There was no need to bring attention to her breasts or hips. Her clothes were still attractive and made of nice fabrics, but without all the ornaments that most women preferred.

"I don't believe you've ever officially met my dear husband." Lena pulled the slightly rotund, balding man to her side. "This is my Henry." She kissed him on the cheek. "Darling, this is Vivian March. She has an impeccable reputation as the very best lady in town."

"A pleasure, Miss March," he said.

Vivian noted the genuine look of kindness etched on his round face. They were not a particularly attractive couple, but a well put-together couple. When standing next to each other, their love shone so brightly it made up for any aesthetic shortcomings.

Once upon a time she had thought she had found a love match such as theirs, but she'd been a fool. Now she knew the truth, both from her own experience and from sweeping London's secrets beneath plush parlor rugs for the last several years, that love was exceptionally rare.

The four of them visited a few additional moments,

mostly discussing the recent rains, and then dinner was announced. Vivian had spent a great deal of time fussing over where everyone would sit at her sixteen-place table. She had carefully placed each guest so that the maximum amount of conversation could be had to keep gossip at a minimum. One of those arrangements had been to seat Clarissa next to Mr. Rodale, something she knew would greatly annoy Clarissa, but it was something that had to be done. If it appeared to those in attendance tonight that the two of them had been acquaintances for a number of years because of her brother, then it would ease people's concerns as to why she'd been in such a place of ill repute.

Clarissa shot her a glare as they were seated. Vivian pretended to misinterpret and merely smiled back. She had been quite strategic for herself, though, and had placed Marcus as far away from her as possible. Instead, she'd put Mr. Rodale next to her, then Clarissa after him and on her other side, Vivian had seated Lena's husband.

It was an interesting mixture, this dinner party, but tonight would be a success. Already she knew the matrons, as well as the misses she'd included, had warmed to Mr. Rodale's handsome face and charming demeanor. He might not be a nobleman, but he certainly knew how to converse with them. Vivian had done her research and knew fundamental information about him. He was the illegitimate son of the Duke of Chanceworth, though now his half-brother held that title. But he'd been educated with the rest of the aristocrats, had gone to Cambridge, and then Justin Rodale had used his education and contacts to build the most opulent and profitable gaming establishment in all of London.

But Marcus was all the rage. The ladies flirted with him

while the men exchanged jests. This was a small portion of London's elite, but she had strategically selected the attendees knowing full well they'd pass on the details of the night the most effectively. So far, things were going precisely as she'd planned.

Once the first course was served the questions for Marcus began. "Oh, do tell us about your most recent adventure, Lord Ashford," Lady Aldridge asked.

"Or, better still, tell us the most dangerous," Viscount Danford suggested.

All eyes were on Marcus, but his locked on hers. "Very well, I'll tell a few stories, but I do not wish to take away from Miss March. This is her party."

"In your honor, my lord," she said with a nod. "People came to welcome you back to London. They want to hear your stories."

Marcus couldn't help but notice how far he sat from the illustrious Miss March. He was no fool. She'd put him over here on purpose. Of course, she'd also seated him near two of the most notorious gossips in all of London, at least according to Aunt Maureen. All it had taken was a couple of well-placed compliments and smiles, and they were both fawning all over him. Some women were so easy, too easy, while others proved to be quite the challenge.

He eyed his hostess down the length of the table and she smiled. They wanted him to tell his stories. She'd been right. This was precisely what she'd said they would do. He settled on which story to tell and cleared his throat. "We took a group, a small group, mostly men, to Africa. They had wanted to see all the exotic animals. There we were all in a handful of boats traveling down the Tana River, and crocodiles were everywhere, sunning themselves on the muddy banks and swimming beside the boats."

"That sounds positively terrifying," Lady Forrester said. She placed her hand on Marcus's arm. "However did you manage to be so brave?"

"We were well armed." That got him a round of laughs. He caught Vivian's glance and she gave him a small nod of reassurance.

"Go on, then," Viscount Danford said.

"We were getting closer to where we would camp for the night and then we saw them." He shook his head for emphasis. "Serious danger."

"What sort of danger?" Lord Forrester asked.

"Was it a lion?" Clarissa asked. Marcus eyed his sister, momentarily surprised she too was curious about the expedition. It was the first time since his return that she'd looked at him with an expression other than one filled with resentment.

"No, I'll bet it was a particularly large crocodile," Lady Garner said before Marcus could answer.

"Worse," Marcus said. "Bubbles came up to the surface of the river, all around us." He used his hands to demonstrate, as if they all sat in a boat instead of at a table in an opulent dining room. "We were surrounded."

"By bubbles?" Viscount Danford asked.

"Hippopotamus," Marcus said.

One of the younger ladies giggled. "But they're so cute with their little ears. I've seen pictures of them. At the museum."

"Cute, perhaps," Marcus said, holding up one finger. "But deadly. They're vicious and we were surrounded."

"Oh dear, however did you get out?" Lady Forrester asked.

Marcus shrugged. "We tossed over a particularly annoying fellow to engage them, then the rest of us paddled as fast as we could."

"You did not," Clarissa said. "That would be dreadful." She actually smiled at him.

"You're right, dear sister. We didn't do that, but we did fire a few warning shots into the water and then paddled as quickly as we could. We got out of the water safely and made our camp for the night."

"How do you keep the animals away at night?" This question came from Vivian. He had begun to wonder if she was paying any attention to his tale.

"We had guards and we took turns. And as I said, we had guns. Plenty of them. And we lit fires that surrounded the campsites."

"Sounds horrifically dangerous," Lady Garner said.

"Sounds exciting," Justin said.

"It's all of those things. I won't lie and say we haven't had any injuries or close calls, but we do our best to keep it as safe as possible for people."

"Would you go back?" Viscount Danford asked.

"Of course. I've been to Africa many times, to many countries within—Egypt and Morocco. I've also traveled to the Orient and India and many places in between."

"The animals don't frighten you?" Again it was Vivian who asked.

"Some of them do." He smiled. "I'm not particularly fond of snakes or scorpions. They can be quite nasty. But you learn to shake out your clothes and shoes."

Again a round of laughter. Everyone was entranced. He hadn't expected her plan to work, but he'd be the first to admit she had been right. Of course, this was but a small gathering of London's finest. There were more people to deal with, and he knew the worst of this situation wasn't over yet. But protecting Clarissa was the most important thing for him to do now. He had walked out on his family once, and he wouldn't do that again. Once Clarissa was married off, he'd be free to return to his life as before. But until then he'd do what he could to protect her.

The rest of the dinner party flew by in a flurry of questions, with him telling story after story of his adventures. He didn't mind it; he enjoyed his travels. It was one of the reasons he'd sought out the position with Thomas Adventure Tours.

Again and again, as he spoke, he found his eyes drawn to the woman at the end of the table. Her sable gaze had stayed on him, but as soon as he'd meet it she'd look away, turn to the person next to her to ask a question, or she'd take a sip of her drink. Anything, it seemed, but lock eyes with him.

He unsettled her, he could see that. It wasn't so much that he made her nervous—Vivian March seemed to have a strong constitution—but he knew she was constantly aware of him. He rather liked that fact. It meant that she, quite likely, was as attracted to him as he was to her.

There were other women to be had in London. Just this evening he'd received a handful of suggestive glances from the women in attendance, two of whom were already married. But it was Vivian March who had captured his interest. There was simply something about her, something he couldn't ignore. And he wanted to speak to her tonight. Alone.

He enjoyed her conversation, the tone of her voice. It was her proper way and he wanted nothing more than to make her stumble. Not literally, but merely in her thoughts. Wanted to trip her up, catch her off guard. Get her to say more things that she hadn't meant to say. That was when people were the most honest.

As the guests began to depart he made a point of leaving his sister conversing with two other women in the party. Vivian stood near the door saying goodbye. Then he motioned for Clarissa and Lena and Henry to make their way to the carriage.

"Henry, be a good sport and see the ladies to the carriage. I need a word with Miss March and I shall be right behind you," Marcus said.

"Very good," Henry said as he led the women out the door.

"Why are you not leaving?" Vivian asked as his party left him standing alone with her.

"I wanted to speak with you. Privately."

She glanced around them to ensure no one had heard him. "That's not a good idea."

"I promise not to ravish you." He arched his brows. "At least, not tonight."

"You are incorrigible and remarkably inappropriate," she said, though her tone did not suggest she was all that scandalized by his behavior. "If you will excuse me," she said to the other guests, "I am going to see Lord Ashford out." They walked out into the hall and she opened her study door. "We are alone now. If we must speak privately, you could at the least tell me whether or not you think tonight was a success, or do you still believe my plan to be an utter failure?"

He smiled and nodded in concession. "Yes, I do think tonight was a success. I admit that perhaps you know what you are talking about. You certainly understand these people more than I do." He wanted to touch her, but he knew if he reached out too soon, she'd spook. Much like the prey alerted to the hunter that stalked nearby. "I've traveled with aristocrats, but that is different. Out there, in the wilds of a dangerous land, they must rely on me and the other guards to keep them safe. They can't afford to behave in their usual entitled fashion."

"I'm glad you can admit when you're wrong," she said with a nod. "It's a rare trait."

"Rare in men, or people in general?"

"People in general, but men in particular." She smiled a genuine smile that struck him right in the gut.

"You were the loveliest woman here tonight," he said.

"I see you have other traits, of charming and lying, as well."

"I'm not lying. I never lie when it comes to speaking of a woman's beauty. And with you, the lie would have been unnecessary."

She chuckled, then perhaps realized from his expression that he was telling the truth. "Thank you."

"And I see you, too, can admit when you're wrong. I've wanted to do this all night."

He pulled her to him and pressed his mouth down on hers. His lips slanted across hers, and it took very little coaxing to get her to respond. Her tongue stroked against his, and desire thundered through him. He held her against him and kissed her with every ounce of passion he felt. Her response was intoxicating, so heated and unrestrained. He couldn't get enough. He deepened the kiss, and he could have sworn he heard her sigh.

He wanted to toss her onto the floor and plow into her.

She pressed her hands against his chest and pushed him away. "That will be quite enough."

"You should stop being so tempting if you want me to stop kissing you."

"You need to control your urges. Good evening, my lord," she said and he knew in no uncertain terms he'd been dismissed.

He toyed with the idea of kissing her hand, but didn't want to push her too far tonight. Instead, he bowed slightly. "Until the next time, Miss March."

As he walked to the waiting carriage, he replayed their kiss. Her reaction had been perfect. She might claim to not want his advances, but her kisses spoke otherwise. Her passion was intoxicating, exhilarating, and potentially addictive.

Yes, kissing Vivian was most assuredly dangerous.

But Marcus loved danger.

Chapter Five

Marcus stood next to the table and with a flick of his hands unrolled the collection of maps. He set paperweights at each corner, and then stood back to survey his work. He didn't need to look at the maps because he'd already memorized the routes he'd created.

Thomas Adventure Tours: Around the World. They'd be the first touring company to offer such a trip. It had been weeks since he'd submitted his itinerary, carefully planned out over weeks of poring over these same maps in dimly lit tents leading that last tour in Africa. But no word yet from Mr. Thomas and which itinerary they'd selected.

He stared at the map so long it became a blur of lines and curves. Even if he was selected to lead the tour, he didn't know if he could leave. He wanted to, that much he knew. But he wasn't so heartless as to recognize that whether his sister knew it or not, she needed him. So he couldn't simply desert her. At least, not yet. While he was eager to hear from

Mr. Thomas, he recognized that it wasn't a bad thing that word hadn't yet come.

He focused again on the maps. The one on top was of America, where he'd proposed a stagecoach journey from the east to the west coast. It seemed that nothing fascinated aristocrats more than the wilds of the American west, with tales of gold and silver mines, problems with Indians, and gunfights in the middle of the streets. It was well populated, but seemed untamed and uncivilized, and to the genteel population of London, it was a source of endless intrigue.

"Are you planning a visit to the Americas?" Clarissa asked from the other side of the table.

Only a short amount of time in London and already his instincts were fading. He hadn't heard her approach. That would not have been good had she been a wild cat or a native carrying a sharp weapon.

"Not precisely. This is a route I mapped out for a special holiday that Mr. Thomas wants to provide." He stepped around the table, diverting her attention from his maps. "Did you need something?"

She wandered over to the leather chairs opposite his desk. Marcus followed her and sat in the chair adjacent to hers.

"I was wondering if perhaps you might make a better effort to be kind to George," she said.

"I have not even met him, and he has made no effort in remedying that situation. I may have been out of London for a while, but I do believe it is still important for a man courting a woman to seek out the men in her family for approval."

She set her jaw. "So you will not even walk up to him

and introduce yourself?"

"I will not." Marcus tried to soften his voice. "Clarissa, this man has done nothing, as far as I can tell, to indicate he has any intentions that lean toward courtship, let alone marriage, with you. Yes, he dances with you, but so do Lord Blankenship and Justin, as well as a whole host of other men."

"We walk together every Wednesday in the park," she said defensively.

"And how long has that been a tradition?" he asked.

She sucked in a quick breath. "Perhaps eight months or so. We have been friends for a while."

"Eight months, and yet he has not made formal intentions of courtship known. Clarissa, the man has no interest in marrying you."

Her eyes widened. "You do not know him."

"No, but I am a man. If he wanted to marry you, he would have asked already." The bastard was going to hurt his sister and that was not to be tolerated, at least if Marcus could help it. "From now on I do not want you to spend any time with him."

"You cannot do that."

"I can and I will. I am quite serious, Clarissa. No more time with this Wilbanks man. If, as you say, he is prepared to offer for your hand, he will come speak to me. But no more walks, no more dancing, none of it. Am I understood?" She could hate him now, but eventually she would see that this was the best decision for her.

"I am not a child," she said, coming to her feet.

"No, but you are my sister and it is my duty to protect you. This is the only way I know how to do so."

"You are a cretin."

"Perhaps," he said.

"And if I disobey?"

"We shall retire to the country for an extended stay. I'm told that Ashford Manor could use some attention."

She stared at him for several moments, her chest rising and falling quickly in her anger. Then she turned on her heel and left.

She'd already been angry with him, but this was something that had to be done. In the meantime, he might consider finding out which club George Wilbanks frequented so he could have a conversation with him. Tell the bastard to stay the hell away from his sister.

• • •

Vivian had gone over the speech in her head several times already that morning. Then she'd practiced once again in the carriage on the way to his townhouse. Now that she was waiting for him, she knew precisely what to say and how to lead into it. This was a delicate matter, but it had to be handled. She could no longer allow Marcus to continue to take liberties with her, especially since she seemed to have no defenses against his advances. It seemed as though, once he was in the room with her, she completely forgot what she was about, what she'd stood for these past ten years. He'd nearly made her forget her own name with his wicked kisses!

She paced across the Persian rug in his front parlor waiting for him to appear. She had specifically told the butler she wanted to see him alone. This would, hopefully, be the last time that they were alone, but it was most assuredly a conversation they needed to have in private.

"Miss March," he purred as he stepped into the room. "You wanted to see me in private." He flashed her a wicked smile and walked toward her. "I appreciate your boldness."

She held her hand up. "Please do not come any closer. I find that you have cast some sort of wicked spell over me, which prevents me from thinking clearly. But it stops today." She cut her hand across her palm for emphasis. "I've come to discuss something of utmost importance with you."

"Very well, let us sit." He motioned to the chairs behind them. "I admit I am eager for what it is you've come to say."

She sat and then took great care straightening her skirt. Despite her rehearsals this morning of how to discuss this with him, admittedly she was somewhat nervous, which truly made no sense. She had had countless discussions far more difficult than this with any number of other gentlemen. "Well, then, allow me to come right out with it, as it were. You need a wife."

"Miss March, this is all so forward." He braced his hand on his chest to look taken aback. "I'm flattered, truly, but we've only known each other a few days." He grinned, as if enjoying his own jest.

She snorted. "You are hilarious."

He gave her a mock bow. "Thank you,"

"I, however, am quite serious, Marcus. You *need* a wife and I intend to find you one. It will be the perfect diversion away from your sister's scandal. Once the word is out that you are looking for a wife, all the marriageable misses and their mothers will turn their attention to that instead of worrying about poor Clarissa and her conversation with Mr. Rodale. Another available earl—and this one with money."

She smiled. "Honestly, I don't know why I didn't think of it before."

"I don't want a wife." He stretched his long legs out in front of him as if daring her to look. Which, of course, she did because they appeared impossibly long encased in his black trousers and how was it even possible she could see the muscular nature of his thighs? She averted her eyes quickly.

She shook her head. "Every man wants a wife. Every man needs a wife."

"That is a completely false statement."

"Is it? I don't think so. Perhaps you, the adventurer, didn't need a wife. But you are an earl now, and you must have a wife—you need an heir." She waved her hand. "It's bound to happen sooner or later, and I'm the perfect person to select a bride for you. I know all of the available women, and I can give you the details on them."

"I take back what I said before about your previous plan. *This* is the foolish plan."

"I don't believe it is."

He came to his feet so that he towered over her. "Don't think I don't know the real reason you are doing this."

"Because you need a wife, I told you," Vivian said. She crossed her arms over her chest as she looked up at him.

"No, you're doing this—" He leaned over, bracing his hands on the arms of her chair, effectively pinning her into her seat. He looked directly into her eyes. "—because you think it will keep me away from you." His glance dropped to her mouth and he licked his lips.

Vivian wasn't certain if her corset was too tight or if she was nearing a swoon, but it suddenly felt difficult to breathe.

She watched his tongue slide across his bottom lip and she bit down on hers to keep her own mouth closed.

He leaned in close and whispered against her ear. "You think it will keep me from kissing you."

She shivered in response and knew her breath caught.

Again he looked into her eyes. "But know this, Vivian March. Finding me a wife isn't going to distract me from pursuing you. I'm coming after you, so you had best prepare yourself."

Coming after her.

What did that mean? And why the devil was she currently feeling so bloody alive? She should be furious at his roguish behavior! She was certainly intent on finding him a wife. Tomorrow Clarissa and her aunt would come for a visit and together they would create a list of potential brides for him. This matchmaking was going to happen despite his efforts otherwise. Once he saw the beautiful young women eager to be on his arm, he'd forget all about this ridiculous idea of seducing her.

Vivian would be a liar, though, if she didn't admit there was a tiny piece of her that hoped he might be successful. But she knew she'd never allow herself to be seduced again.

The following morning, Vivian closed the door to the front parlor and turned to face her aunt and her two guests. "I'm so pleased you could join me this morning. We have a most important task ahead of us, ladies, so I felt it best for all of us meet."

Clarissa and her Aunt Maureen sat beside one another on the pale green settee. "Your note was most urgent," Clarissa said. Then her hand went to her throat. "Oh dear, have the rumors begun?"

For the first time, the girl seemed truly concerned about the predicament in which she'd placed herself. Vivian waved her hand. "No, no, nothing of the sort. This meeting is entirely about your brother."

Clarissa visibly relaxed. "Boorish, isn't he?"

"Well, I—that is to say, I believe he needs a wife." She wasn't going to detail all that had transpired between herself and Marcus with his sister and aunt, so she used another excuse. "A feminine hand will soften his rougher edges—civilize him, so to speak." Not to mention, she herself was so weak, she feared she'd need him married off so she wouldn't succumb to temptation.

"Excellent plan, my dear," Aunt Rose said. "But match-making, Vivian? Need I remind you about the time you attempted to convince Miss Rosewood to set her cap for Viscount Tilton?"

Vivian shook her head. "No, I'm still trying to forget." Then she started to giggle.

"Someone had to *convince* her to set her cap for him?" Clarissa asked. "Oh, you simply must tell us the story."

Vivian looked at the faces surrounding her, smiling, expectant. "He seemed lonely and she was not as yet married and it seemed like a good idea at the time. So I gently suggested to her that she make it known to him she would welcome his attentions."

"She not only let him know, but the rest of London as

well," Rose said.

"Yes, well, the girl evidently has no understanding of subtlety. And poor Viscount Tilton, every time he sees me, he glares at me. And it's been two years. Do you know she is still following him around? Poor girl tries to hide herself behind trees and lamp posts."

Aunt Maureen laughed. "Her mother should keep a closer watch on her."

"Yes, well, evidently he had attempted courtship when she'd first been introduced into society, but it had gone very poorly," Vivian said.

Aunt Rose smiled. "There was no possible way you could have known they'd had a past. He'd kept that secret for a while."

"And for good reasons, it seems," Vivian said. She was so accustomed to knowing people's secrets that it always came as a bit of a shock if someone had one with which she was unfamiliar. "Nor could I have known how obsessive she is. Or perhaps I should say possessive. It is no wonder the girl is still unmarried." Vivian smoothed her skirts.

"That was only one, though," Clarissa said. "Have you tried to match other couples?"

"Should I tell them about the time you tried to match Henrietta and Finley?" her aunt asked with a grin.

Vivian held up her hand, but could not keep herself from smiling, too. "I maintain that is a perfectly made match. How was I supposed to know they were already a couple? No one knew they had eloped. But clearly I could see how well they went together. That is a success story."

Clarissa clapped her hands. "Oh, that is too perfect."

"Vivian, love, with all your talents," Rose said, shaking

her head, "perhaps there is an alternative solution here."

"No, matchmaking it is. But those previous situations were precisely the reason I have called in reinforcements." Vivian smiled warmly at Clarissa and Maureen. "Though he has been away for many years, you two lovely ladies know Marcus the best. Not only that, but you both have splendid ties in society, and I have no doubt you'll have some suggestions." She withdrew a small notebook from the table beside her, along with a pencil. "Now then, shall we begin making our list?"

"A list?" Maureen asked. "Of what?"

"Potential brides for your nephew, of course," Vivian said.

"I do not know my brother very well, but I can tell you he will be most reluctant to be married off to some girl," Clarissa said.

"Be that as it may," Vivian said, "you must have some friends or acquaintances, Clarissa, who would be a good match for your brother."

"To be honest, Miss March, I'm not so certain I wish to saddle any of my friends with a man whom I can't guarantee will be here when she might need him."

"Clarissa," Maureen chided. "He's simply been gone so long." Maureen opened her mouth as if to say more, but she shook her head.

"You believe your brother will leave again?" Vivian asked.

"Well, I do believe he is still exchanging correspondence with his employer. I don't believe he's ended his position with them, and he certainly spends enough time studying all the maps that litter his desk."

Marcus returning to his post was not something Vivian

had considered. Why would she think about that? Surely he hadn't entertained such thoughts. He was an earl now, he had familial responsibilities he couldn't walk away from. But regardless of all of that, the man needed a wife. What happened after he married would no longer be her concern.

"All the more reason to distract him with a lovely young woman who will steal his attention." Anything that would divert his attention enough to keep him from looking at her with those sultry blue eyes, or pulling her against him in another soul-searing kiss. She couldn't take much more of it. A woman's restraint could only withstand so much temptation. But she was not the right woman to distract him; she was far too advanced in years. She had to be at least six years older than he.

He needed a wife, and she had no desire to be said wife. Or anyone's wife, for that matter. She much preferred living life on her own terms.

"What about Gwyneth Montrose?" Maureen said, finally offering up a name. "She's lovely and seems rather intelligent."

"True, and we know each other, but we aren't close enough that I would need to feel guilty should he abandon her once the marriage is done," Clarissa said thoughtfully.

"Very good," Vivian said. She wrote down Gwyneth's name and tried to place the girl. If she wasn't mistaken, Gwyneth was a relatively tall woman with nondescript brown hair, but kind eyes. She wasn't overly talkative and seemed to have a pleasant disposition. Perhaps *she* was the right sort of woman for Marcus. But Vivian knew even as she wrote the woman's name down that Marcus would no more be interested in her than he would be paying court to Her Majesty.

"Very well. Whom else should we consider? We should have a collection of women to introduce him to. Allow him to select one that interests him, " Vivian said.

"Make him feel as if he's making the choice," Rose said.

"Precisely," Vivian agreed.

"Oh, what about Constance Brindwell?" Clarissa asked. "She's very pretty. And sophisticated."

Not to mention a bit of a flirt, if rumors were to be believed, but Vivian kept that notion to herself. She wrote the woman's name down. They needed good choices for him, someone who would help him lead the Kincaid family, someone to whom Clarissa could look for womanly advice, though clearly she had her aunt for some of that.

"Annie Liddle," Maureen said. "She's very quiet, but a pretty little thing."

She was indeed quite pretty. Perhaps too pretty, but Vivian wrote her name down as well. What did it matter to her if Marcus married himself off to the prettiest woman in all of London? In all of Great Britain, for that matter. She cared not a whit about any of that. She did not want his attention, and this was precisely what needed to happen to prevent him from giving it to her.

Once he had a real marital candidate in his sights he'd forget about Vivian. She was older than he. Gray had already begun to shimmer in her brown hair, and lines had begun to play at the corners of her eyes. Men, especially men like Marcus, did not want women with age showing. They wanted younger, plump, ripe women who were ready to birth children. Vivian was past that part of her life. She was nearing five and thirty, for heaven's sake.

"Eloise Jennings," Clarissa said. "We were friends once,

but lost touch, and she was always very humorous. Marcus enjoys a good laugh, I do know that about him. I suspect Eloise might amuse him."

Vivian wrote down the girl's name. She'd never had any encounters with Eloise, which she supposed was a good thing considering Vivian's particular skill. The less she knew someone, the more likely it was the person had had no personal scandals.

Marcus did seem to have a rather advanced sense of humor. She certainly didn't consider humor as one of her virtues. Oh, what did it matter? She nearly smacked her thigh with the small notebook to shock herself out of her wistful thinking. The point was to get good ideas about whom to introduce Marcus to at his first big ball since his return.

A handful of other names were tossed around and Vivian wrote them all down. They discussed the group and made some additional notes. "Clarissa, did you bring the invitations as I asked?"

"I did." The girl reached into her bag and withdrew a pile of envelopes. "These are for this coming week."

"Excellent. Now let us make our plan to see which would be most advantageous for Marcus to attend. If he is to meet a lovely lady and begin courting her, we want that to happen as soon as possible. Then you, dear Clarissa, may return to your regular activities." She paused and pointed her pencil at the girl. "Though I would suggest steering clear of Mr. Rodale's gambling establishment."

"I have no desire to see Mr. Rodale again," Clarissa said firmly.

"You know that's not really an option right now, my dear. Remember, he is a close family friend. He will in all likelihood be attending some of these functions with you and your brother," Vivian said. "We must keep up appearances."

"Indeed," Clarissa said, then her lips tightened and she said nothing more.

Vivian couldn't help but wonder precisely what had gone on between Mr. Rodale and Clarissa. After the women had left, she reviewed the list of names scrawled into her notebook. With the plan firmly in hand, she knew the very next step was to give Marcus some practical instructions. He'd been gone from London for too long.

She stood at the window and watched the women be ushered into their waiting carriage. They rolled off and Vivian almost walked away, but a flash of black caught her attention. There, across the street, sat that same rig she'd spotted the other day—same worn-out crest, same face peering out from the widow. Vivian stepped away from her own window, her hands shaking.

Well, this was ridiculous. She marched herself out her front door with every intention of walking over to the carriage and confronting whoever found her so fascinating. But as soon as she reached the sidewalk, the carriage rolled away.

It was alarming, yet rather curious.

Chapter Six

Marcus had been summoned to Vivian's townhouse shortly after luncheon. He was led to her formal parlor where he found her already seated. The chair she sat upon appeared to be out of place, though, perhaps brought in from another room. Whereas the rest of the furniture looked plush, her wooden straight-backed chair kept her sitting completely upright.

"Vivian," he said with a nod. "Are you redecorating?"

She gave him a sly smile. "No, I only recently refashioned this room."

"For a woman so concerned with propriety, you certainly are comfortable meeting with me, an eligible bachelor, alone. Are you not concerned for your virtue?"

"A woman of my advanced years need not concern herself with the worries of a younger woman."

"Advanced years—honestly, Vivian, you make yourself sound as if you have one foot in the grave. Trust me, your virtue could be in even more danger now," he said.

She inhaled sharply. "Lord Ashford, let us try and stay on task. This chair is here for a specific reason, but I am thrilled to see that you are so visually observant and noticed it was a new addition to the room. Trust me when I say that it will make this exercise go much more smoothly."

"Exercise? I am intrigued." He sat nearest her, on a cream-colored oval-backed chair.

"There is much you need to learn about wooing a lady and winning her hand."

"Is that what this is going to be about?" He sat back, utterly amused by her. He would say one thing—she never ceased to amaze him with her antics, especially since she was completely sincere. "You intend to teach me how to court a lady?"

"Well, not today—there is much to discuss before we actually get to the courtship," she said. "Remember, it is always good to learn new things."

"Consider me a most attentive pupil," he said.

"Excellent. Let us begin, then. I know that you have been out of the country for much of your formative years. Therefore, I suspect some of the fairer sex's cues are lost on you." It was then that he saw the fan hanging from her wrist.

"Cues? Vivian, to what are you referring?"

She withdrew her wrist from the loop of the fan and popped it open on her thigh. "In order to find a bride, you will need to know what subtle messages women are sending you. In the delicate language of the fan, for instance."

He grinned, unable to help it. "There is a language of the fan? And a covert language, at that." He released a low whistle. "The queen really ought enlist some women to serve in the espionage department. You lot are a clever bunch."

"Yes, well, don't allow our secret to escape. Were it known that we actually could do everything, you men would stop earning your keep. Now then—" She held the fan up to her face, staring at him over its blade coquettishly. "There is much a woman can say to you with only her fan." She dropped the fan and waved it quickly in front of her. "See how rapidly I am fanning myself? This means I am engaged. If I slow it down, it means I am already married."

He leaned back in the chair and watched her. This was going to be a most interesting afternoon. She might not have realized it, but this little exercise was allowing Vivian to flirt with him, and he found that to be most entertaining.

"This," she said, opening and closing the fan, "means that I find you cruel. But this," she said, touching the closed fan to her right ear, "means that you have changed."

"For better or worse?"

"I suppose that depends on the individuals involved." She continued moving the fan about and it all seemed a ridiculous means of communication to him, but he found her charming.

She was intent on finding him a bride, and he had to wonder what it was about him that ruffled her so. Vivian was no longer a young miss on the marriage mart. She was a woman of means old enough to make decisions of her own. She had no men in her life dictating her every move. Why, then, was she so reluctant to give in to her own desires? He knew she wanted him. Her fan might be saying otherwise— at the moment she was telling him she despised him—but her eyes said something else entirely.

"This means I want to speak to you alone." She moved

the fan so that the handle touched her lips. "And that means I want a kiss."

"I want a kiss, too," he said.

"Marcus, be serious, will you?"

"I was being quite serious. I never jest about kissing."

She shook her head fervently. "It is important to remember that even if a woman makes such a gesture, you mustn't give in to every girl who makes the request. There are plenty of lightskirts out there doing everything in their power to compromise themselves into a marriage with a titled gentleman."

"This all seems nothing but nonsense to me."

"Oh no, women can be quite crafty. Marriage is highly competitive in London. There are only so many handsome men who have other fine attributes such as your title and your wealth. Women will do what they can to make such a match, so as to not be saddled with an older gentleman with soured breath, despite his title and full coffers."

"That's not what I meant," he said. He leaned forward, bracing his elbows on his knees. "It seems foolish that women would have to come up with such a creative way to speak to a man. Would it not be more simple for her say what she wants?"

"Oh, no, that would be unheard of. Improper, really. A woman should never admit to a man that she wishes he would court her or that she wants a kiss. Nor should she tell a man she believes him to be cruel. This is polite society, after all." She placed the fan on the occasional table next to her.

"We all certainly pretend to be polite quite well. It is so much simpler with animals. Do you know that when a lioness is ready to mate, she simply rolls around on the ground growling, and the male lion comes and mounts her? It's that simple."

Vivian's mouth had fallen open. Her breathing had tightened and her hands clenched the fabric of her skirt. He had obviously scandalized her with his information, but was it possible that he had aroused her as well? The very thought had lust surging through his veins, making his trousers uncomfortable.

Vivian recovered quickly. She frowned. "That is not the type of conversation you should have with any of the girls you will be courting. Highly improper. And Marcus, honestly, we are not wild animals. You cannot compare the two. If women went about rolling on the floor and moaning all the time with men coming along and mounting them, as you so crudely called a ball, Society would be no better than orgies I've heard about. We are civilized, educated people. We know better."

"Yes, we do. Still, it would be a vast improvement if women could speak their desires aloud rather than using some antiquated code." He had forgotten how different Englishwomen were from women elsewhere. Vivian was very much a proper Englishwoman, so very intelligent, yet she could be somewhat naïve when it came to matters of the flesh.

"Be that as it may, knowing these things will assist you in finding the right girl."

He knew the futility of arguing with her. Vivian had set her course, though he would not agree to stay on it with her, but there was no point in discussing it. Instead, he had other matters to converse about.

"You are a most fascinating woman, Vivian March."

Clearly uncomfortable with his straightforward compliment, she merely smiled and patted her hair.

"Join me for dinner tonight at Lena and Henry's," he said.

The lines between her brow furrowed. "I cannot."

"And why is that?"

"I am busy." She waved her hand in front of her. "I am behind on our books. And I really must go through our mail."

He eyed the small stack of letters on the writing desk behind her. Crossing his arms over his chest, he raised his eyebrows. "Give me a specific reason and I shall leave you alone." His words carried an open challenge. "I thought you enjoyed my cousin's company."

"Yes, of course, I enjoy your cousin quite a bit."

"I would hate for her feelings to be wounded if you did not attend."

Her eyes narrowed. "Did she invite me?"

"Most assuredly she did. She told me quite specifically to not forget to invite you," he said. It wasn't true, but had Lena known he was going to see Vivian today, she most certainly would have said those very words.

She was quiet for several moments, then a slow smile spread across her mouth. "I am rather fond of your cousin. I haven't seen Lena in a while, and I didn't get to visit with her much the other night. I suppose I could accompany you."

That was far easier than he had anticipated. Vivian had a plan, ulterior motives, he would wager. He suspected she intended to persuade his cousin to her plan of marrying him off, but he said nothing of the matter. It would be far more entertaining to watch how it played out, see what kinds of schemes she planned.

She came to her feet and moved toward the door, ready to see him out. He followed her over and stood too close to her. Her breath caught at his nearness. He suspected she wondered if he would kiss her again.

"I shall send a carriage for you," he said.

"Marcus, I'm not so certain it's a great idea for us to spend time alone with one another."

He leaned down and pressed a lingering kiss on her cheek. "You have my word that I will not touch you. I shall be a perfect gentleman. Tonight." He would not make promises for any other evening. He still wanted her. This afternoon had already been an exercise in restraint. Her lessons in flirting had him longing for a time when she would ask him, just once, to kiss her. Even if she did have to do it with a bloody fan.

"Vivian, dear, the carriage is here!" Aunt Rose called.

Vivian rounded the corner of the stairs into the main foyer. She walked directly to her aunt and held her wrist out. "Fasten this, please." Rose busied herself with the bracelet encircling Vivian's wrist.

"He said he'd wait outside," Rose said.

He had promised to be the gentleman, she reminded herself, trying to calm her nerves. She didn't know if she was more concerned about him kissing her or not kissing her. "He is right on time. I find that somewhat surprising."

"Because handsome men cannot be prompt?" Aunt Rose looked up from the clasped bracelet.

"I never once said he was handsome."

"You didn't have to, dear. By the by, you look very pretty this evening." Rose smiled. "I'm going to retire early, so do not expect me to still be awake when you return."

"Aunt Rose, I am going to dinner. I will not be out late."

"Nonetheless, do not disturb me." She kissed Vivian's cheek. "Have a good time, dear."

Vivian made her way out the front door and couldn't help but notice as she walked past the mirror in the entryway that the rich indigo did complement her skin tone.

He stood by the street, next to the carriage, the crest of Ashford emblazoned on the side of the rig. His clothes spoke to all the wealth and privilege of his family, yet when he reached out to help her climb into the carriage, she noted he still did not wear gloves.

"I hope you're hungry," he said as the doors closed on them. "If memory serves me right, Lena and Henry always have the very best dishes at their house."

She was hungry, though she hadn't given much thought to the actual dinner part of the evening. She'd been mostly concerned with being alone with him in here. As the wheels began to rumble down the street, she was quite relieved that Marcus had sat across from her.

They were quiet for several moments before Marcus spoke. "Lions mate on and off for nearly three days solid," he said.

"I beg your pardon?" she asked.

"You seemed—" He paused as if looking for the right word. "—intrigued when I told you some of the mating rituals of lions. I thought you might be curious to know more. The actual act of coupling doesn't last very long, so they do it often, not even taking breaks to eat or hunt. They're quite serious about their mating."

She hadn't been so much intrigued as aroused by his earlier description, and he had noticed. Heat settled in her cheeks and she knew she blushed. Thanks goodness the carriage was relatively dark as they rumbled down the street.

"The male lion is quite attentive to his female when she's ready for breeding. I suspect human males are not too much different. When we see a female we want, we can be pretty attentive. Take myself, for example. My attraction to you has consumed much of my thoughts."

She sucked in her breath. She should say something, chide him or ask him not to say such things, but she found she had no words.

"Vivian, if you only knew the images my mind has conjured of the two of us. Your response to my kisses is, I know, merely an indication of how passionate you are. I am longing to know how you would respond if I kissed you elsewhere."

"Where?" she asked, then gasped because she had not intended to say it aloud.

"If I nibbled at that spot beneath your ear where I can see your pulse flicker beneath your skin. Or if I took my sweet time at the inside of your wrist. More than anything, though, right now, I'd like to kneel in front of you and start at your ankles and kiss my way up your legs. I'd first have to peel down those stockings. But then up your legs until I could taste your sweet nectar."

She swallowed hard and took a shuddering breath. His words conjured those same images in her mind, and heat pooled between her legs. Her nipples had hardened and she was close to asking him to do precisely what he'd described. She'd never heard of such a thing.

"Yes, but this is proper English society, despite whatever carnal rituals the primitive tribes might participate in, genteel people would never do such things" she said, in an attempt to hide how his words had affected her.

"Oh, no, that's a custom a great many Englishmen enjoy—and Englishwomen as well," he said.

"I don't believe that."

"Answer me this, Vivian—are you more scandalized or intrigued by the notion?"

She didn't have to answer because the carriage arrived at the Glenfield townhouse and a footman had opened the door as soon as they rolled to a stop. He assisted her out of the carriage, and then Marcus escorted her inside.

"You look beautiful, Vivian," he whispered against her ear as they entered his cousin's home.

"Welcome, welcome." Lena entered the hallway, her face beaming from the smile gracing her lips. "I am so pleased you decided to join us." She embraced Vivian.

"Thank you for inviting me," Vivian said. She did her best to school her features. Marcus had not only spoken of wicked things on the ride here, he'd made her crave said wicked things. She could still feel desire tingling through her body, clinging to her limbs.

"I must confess that for selfish reasons, I am glad you are here. I do hate it when I am the only woman about." She squeezed Vivian to her. "This will even things up a bit. Let us head to the dining room—dinner should be ready, and we can't very well spend the evening in the hall."

"Cousin, we have only just arrived," Marcus said.

"Yes, well, we have much to discuss this evening. Come along, then," Lena said.

They entered the dining room, a modest room equipped with a table tastefully sized to seat no more than six guests. The smells of broiled quail, potatoes, and warm bread engulfed Vivian's senses.

Marcus guided Vivian to a chair. His hand at the small of her back sent warmth spreading through her, doing nothing to ease her arousal. Good heavens, but she was becoming quite the wanton! It was ridiculous that an innocent touch could affect her so. He pulled out her chair.

She was relieved when Marcus sat across the table from her. She didn't think she could have lasted an entire dinner sitting right next to him.

"It smells delicious," Vivian said, trying to turn her thoughts to something else.

"Where is Henry?" Marcus asked.

"In here," Henry said as he bumped a door open. He walked in, all smiles, carrying a tray of food. "Dinner is served." He set the large tray in the center of the table and removed the lid. Four plates sat simmering with mounds of food. "Please, have a seat. Let me just remove this," he said as he untied his apron.

Vivian must have displayed her confusion because Lena raised her eyebrows, then laughed.

"You have discovered our family secret," she said with feigned concern. "It is true, my husband loves to cook. I simply cannot keep him out of the kitchen," Lena said with a laugh.

Vivian felt the heat of a blush crawl up her neck. "I do apologize. I didn't mean to imply—"

"Not at all," Lena said. "It is a normal reaction. Most gentlemen don't even know where to find the kitchen, much less how to fix a pot of tea. But I must admit your expression was delightful." Lena clapped her hands.

Henry served each of them a plate of food, then sat next to Marcus. "Please, eat." Henry picked up his own fork to encourage everyone else.

The aromas of the foods mingled in a most perfect way, beckoning her to taste each dish. Vivian did not believe she had ever had such a wonderful meal. "Good heavens, Henry, but you are a most gifted cook."

"Thank you. It's all in the timing, and I have a penchant for spices."

Marcus cleared his throat, and set his fork down. "You will all be pleased to know that I met with Mr. Thomas this morning. I handed off my upcoming Egyptian tour to another of the guides."

Vivian eyed him. Though his tone seemed relatively neutral, there was a look in his eyes that said something else entirely. She was pleased he was taking his new position seriously and that he was considering staying in London to be with Clarissa. Still, she knew that this decision did not make him happy.

"Splendid, old boy," Henry said. "I'm quite pleased you'll be staying around."

"Have you resigned, then? Completely?" Lena asked, her face lit with joy.

Marcus was quiet for a moment, and then he shook his head. "No, I have not resigned. It has not become completely clear to me that that is necessary. I enjoy my post with Thomas Adventure Tours."

It was the perfect moment to remind him that it didn't matter if he enjoyed his position. Earls did not have paid jobs. And earls did not abandon their younger sisters before they were at the very least married off to a worthy gentleman. But Vivian said nothing. For one, she sensed he knew that. Secondly, he seemed vulnerable enough at the moment that she wasn't certain she wanted to get that close to him. She was completely comfortable giving him advice or guidance in selecting a bride, but anything else would be too much.

"Perhaps we can provide you with another incentive for staying close to home," Lena said. "Henry, may we tell them now?"

"I think now would be a perfect time, darling." Henry went and stood by his wife.

Lena smiled up at Henry, and then looked back at her cousin. "Marcus, I wanted you to be the first to know that Henry and I are expecting our first child."

"Lena, that is wonderful." Marcus came to his feet to embrace his cousin. "I know how long you and Henry have wanted this. I'm so happy for you."

Henry looked every bit the proud father-to-be standing tall next to his wife's chair, eyes glowing, and smiling sweetly at her. And Lena, wiping tears from her eyes, looked truly beautiful. Vivian supposed it was true what people said, that a woman's true beauty shone the brightest when she carried a child.

Vivian rose from her chair and walked to Lena. "How marvelous for both of you. Congratulations."

Lena hugged Vivian tightly. "Thank you."

Something about the whole scene made Vivian's insides knot. She should not be here, to hear such private family news. She had agreed to come tonight in hopes of speaking with Lena about Marcus's marital situation. She thought that if she could have a word alone with the woman, Lena could be a powerful ally in convincing Marcus that marrying was the right thing to do. Instead, she was caught in the middle of an intimate family dinner.

Marcus had obviously invited her to further his plan of seducing her. He wanted her in his bed, but this—this was a family moment and she wanted nothing more than to disappear.

Marcus came and stood behind her and placed his hand at her waist, a touch so familiar it made her knees weak. It was the touch of a lover, a husband, and she was not Marcus's lover and certainly not his wife. This was all wrong. She should not have agreed to come here tonight. She was far too close to this situation, and she never allowed herself to do that with her clients. For this very reason.

Chapter Seven

"I beg your pardon, but where is your water closet?"

"Two doors down to the left. Are you all right, Vivian?" Lena asked. "You look a little pale."

She put her fingers to her temple and gave a weak smile. "I have a bit of a headache and need to splash a little water on my face, that is all. I shall be fine."

Vivian did her best to walk calmly out of the dining room. She felt anything but calm. Instead, her body hummed with anxiety. She did precisely as she'd told them once she was enclosed in the small room. The basin held clean, cool water and she splashed some onto her warm cheeks. This was ridiculous. She didn't have moments like this, not anymore. Now she was the woman who drove the conversation, directed the course of action, defined what was acceptable. She was used to being in charge.

Damnation if she hadn't let her own weakness catch her off guard. Being attracted to Marcus was one thing, but she could not allow him to distract her to such a degree that she forgot whom she'd worked hard to become. She leaned against the closed door. She needed a moment to collect herself. It was apparent that she could not continue to play this charade with Marcus, pretending they could be friends. Men and women could not be friends.

The connection between her and Marcus was too much to deny. No matter how much she tried to ignore it, she knew that Marcus was attracted to her. And she to him. Perhaps he knew the truth about her. Men could probably see right through her, knowing instantly that she was weak and a wanton. Did Marcus know she was not an innocent? Is that why he was so intent on seducing her? Did he know that one touch from him would reduce her to clay in his hands?

She had no legitimate reason for begging off their agreement, save telling him the truth. That could never happen. She could not ignore him, but at least she could prevent herself from being in such intimate positions with him. Not only that, but she could regain control of herself. As traitorous as her body seemed to be, she was master of her own mind, for heaven's sake.

She would see him only in public, surrounded by as many people as possible. She could point out potential brides. Then it was time to retire from society. Perhaps it was time to disappear and allow people to deal with their own scandals for a change. But without a family of her own, the work she did with the families she helped, the reputation she'd built for herself—it was everything she had in the world.

She wiped her face one more time, and pinched her cheeks to bring back the color. With new determination and a stronger will, she returned to the dining room. Henry and Marcus stood as she entered.

"Are you feeling ill, Vivian?" Marcus moved toward her.

She waved him off. "I feel much better now. As I said, it is a small headache, nothing to worry about. I do apologize for leaving in such a manner," she said to Lena.

"Oh, don't be ridiculous. My home is your home."

"Shall we retire to the drawing room?" Henry asked.

Once settled in the large room, Vivian turned to Lena. There was no reason to abandon her plan for the evening. She'd intended to make Lena an ally and she would do that. Henry and Marcus were currently on the other side of the room having a discussion over a large map. "I've decided that the best way to help the family, to take eyes off Clarissa, is to find a bride for Marcus."

Lena raised her eyebrows. "A bride?"

"He's agreed to consider potential women," Vivian said. That wasn't entirely true, but he hadn't said no.

Lena absently rubbed her stomach. "I must admit I'm surprised you convinced him so easily."

"Well, he has only agreed to entertain the idea. I was hoping you might help persuade him to consider the notion of marriage more seriously."

"A wife would certainly go a long way in keeping him in London, or at the very least England." Lena smiled. "Do you have some women in mind?"

Vivian rattled off the list of the girls they'd discussed. "What do you think? Do you know any of them?"

"I do and I think it's a good start." Lena put her hand on Vivian's arm. "I'll consider some other names."

"What are you two whispering about over there?"

Marcus asked from across the room.

"Secrets, dear cousin, delicious secrets," Lena said.

Marcus raised both eyebrows and Vivian couldn't help the chuckle that escaped her. Tonight wasn't a complete loss, after all. She'd still accomplished her goal of talking to Lena, and at the moment Marcus was across the room and not touching her, which was much more conducive to clear thought.

"We were, of course, discussing your future. I know I want to do whatever possible to keep you from leaving us again," Lena said.

Vivian gave her a concerned look, but Lena merely smiled, as if to say, *Trust me.*

Lena walked to the side table next to the sofa and gathered a handful of envelopes. She gave some to Vivian, and then kept the rest for herself. "We can sort through these invitations to see what possibilities we have."

Vivian thought to tell her that she'd already selected balls for them to attend, but if she wanted Lena's assistance, she needed to trust Lena's intuition.

Lena held up an invitation. "This is that masque at the Rampleys', the one you wanted to go to, darling."

"Oh yes. Masques are all the rage," Henry said. "Surely there will be lovely girls there."

Vivian's eyes met Marcus's. "Perhaps a masque isn't the way to go to meet someone for the first time."

"Oh, you're absolutely right," Lena said. "What have you found, Vivian?"

She opened the first envelope. "It is the come-out for Melissa Blair."

"She is a lovely girl," Lena said, "but her mother is a

wretched woman so that will never do. My turn." She opened a cream-colored envelope. "The annual Sanderson soiree. Always a good time, but very few young people in attendance. Vivian?"

"Another come-out. This one is for Lady Judith Hodges. It says here her father is a duke."

"A duke without a fortune." Henry snorted. "I'll bet every decent family in England received an invitation. No doubt looking for a heavy purse for his daughter. Heavy gambler," he said behind his hand.

"I'm so glad all of you find this so amusing," Marcus said. "You discuss my future marriage as though I shall play no part in it."

He hadn't said *potential* marriage; he'd said quite flatly his *future* marriage, as if he'd already resigned himself to the idea. Perhaps she was already getting through to him. Vivian knew this entire task of matchmaking would be infinitely easier if she had a willing groom-to-be.

Marcus watched Vivian close her front door. Neither of them had spoken on the way back to her townhouse. During the ride there he'd wanted to scandalize her, but also let her know how serious his intentions were toward her.

He stood on her steps a few moments longer to try to make sense of the direction his life had suddenly taken. It was the same mental dance he'd done since he'd returned to London. He played everything over again in his mind, wondering what would have happened had he not returned at all. Eventually, word of his inheriting the title would have found him if through no other channels than the family solicitor sending notice through Thomas Adventure Tours.

He returned to his carriage. Everyone around him seemed to want him to stay, and he saw the merits. Right now, though, he was only committing to London until he married off his sister to a decent sort, someone other than that fop she seemed to favor. But marriage…he had never been inclined toward the institution. Both his father and brother had married for love, and it had brought them nothing but heartache and pain. Marcus had seen no reason to pursue matrimony, though clearly now the burden of an heir fell to him. For his entire adult life he'd merely wanted to travel, see the world, and when the occasion called for it, to have a willing woman warm his bed.

He only wanted one woman warming his bed at the moment, and she had just left his carriage. Rather quickly. As if she were afraid of what might happen if they were alone together for too long. Perhaps she should be. Despite her desire to marry him off, he still wanted to seduce her. He found her intriguing, which was why he'd made some subtle inquiries into how she spent her time. She was fascinating, with her skill at hiding other people's scandals, smoothing out the edges of others' indiscretions. It certainly begged the question of when she'd become so skilled at keeping secrets.

He climbed the stairs to his townhouse and made his way to his study. Perhaps someone had gotten back to him regarding his inquiries about Vivian, or he might have received word from Mr. Thomas. It might behoove him to make a visit to the Thomas Adventure Tours office and see if Mr. Thomas had made a decision about the Around the World tours.

There on a silver platter on the top of his desk sat a sealed envelope addressed only to *Kincaid*.

Marcus opened the seal and read the scrawled note.

Before the sun has fully risen. Hyde Park.

He set down the note and smiled. Money well spent to the fellow he'd ask to look into Vivian's past times. He would not have taken her for a rider, but he enjoyed the morning air as well. Maybe if she took his pursuit seriously, she'd give up her silly intentions of finding him a wife.

Early the next morning, as was her custom, Vivian dressed in her riding habit and left early for a ride in the park. It was her time, the only time in the day that was solely hers. She arose too early to meet other people on her journey, so she, along with her groom who rode several paces behind her, could travel through Hyde Park without having to completely conform to society's standards. She rode early so she could ride faster than a lady ought.

It was a lovely morning. The fog had lifted and the sun was beginning to peek gloriously above the trees. Had she been a little earlier she would have had time for a quick canter around, but as it was, she had been a little late this morning and therefore risked encountering other early risers. Usually they were men, quite often, she was certain, coming home from the evening, but she never would have inquired as to such a thing. They would generally nod and tip their hats and off they would go without having to exchange any words.

People knew her, knew that she guarded secrets, though

no one ever dared to speak of it. It was far too risky, this card house of secrets she'd built. One family knew that if they spoke ill of her, she could just as easily share their secret with another family and away the cards would fall.

She heard a rider approaching behind her and wondered if it was her groom riding up to give her a message, but thought better of it. He never bothered her on her ride unless she'd asked him to watch the time, which on this morning, she had not. But the hooves beat a rhythm approaching her and she kept to her side of the path, smoothing her mare's mane to soothe her should she be nervous.

The mystery was soon solved when the rider stopped beside her, slowed his mount, and tipped his hat. "Lovely morning, Miss March," Marcus said.

She frowned at him. "Oh for heaven's sake. Whatever are you doing here?"

"Riding. I've always had a penchant for early morning riding. Clears the head and readies me for the day."

Words that she knew she'd spoken before, though to whom she couldn't recall. He'd known she'd be here, known he could find her on this very path this morning. She wanted to be bothered by the notion of a man following her. Instead, she felt pursued—and as annoying as it was, being pursued felt decidedly delicious. "Have you bribed my servants to give you word of my whereabouts?"

He put a hand to his chest. "Why, Miss March, it wounds me that you would even make such a suggestion. I merely enjoy the park in the morning and I recognized you from behind." He stopped, eyed her, and then slowly smiled. "I wanted to be polite and say hello."

"Well, hello." When he didn't ride off, she motioned with

her hand. "Carry on, then."

"Are you dismissing me?" he asked, his seductive eyes round with feigned innocence.

She nodded. "I am."

"Is my company so dreadful?"

This time she detected a note of truth, perhaps hurt, in his otherwise playful tone. She sighed. "No, of course not. I am not accustomed to riding alongside someone in the morning."

"I shall be quiet. Give you your solitude."

She nodded and he was true to his word. They rode in silence for several long moments, only the sounds of their mounts' hooves against the path and the occasional song of a bird filling their silence. If she were honest with herself, she would admit that it was nice. Riding alongside someone, a companion, without having to speak, without the pressure to say the right thing…but that was not what this was. This was more of his illusions. More of his games.

"Marcus, I do not know what game you wish to play with me, but I can assure you that I will not be a worthy opponent for you."

"I strongly disagree, though I do not believe I am playing a game. Did I not warn you that I was going to pursue you? This is pursuit, my dear lady, not a game. I should think you would recognize the difference."

She took a deep breath. "You are wasting your time."

"Yes, so you have warned me. I should like to be the judge of how I use my time, though."

"Fair enough."

Marcus turned away from Hyde Park and headed his mount in the direction of Brook Street, where the Thomas Adventure Tours office was located. At this early hour it was unlikely Mr. Thomas himself would be in, but his assistant, Mr. Figg, was there so often, Marcus had wondered if the man lived in the back rooms.

And so it was when Marcus arrived. Mr. Figg was just opening up the front door. The little bell at the top of the door jingled as he closed the door behind him. The small office looked the same as he remembered it and still smelled of lemon oil. The heavy wooden desk in the front was where Mr. Figg sat and greeted people. There were a handful of chairs lining the wall to the right for people to wait, and behind the door on the left was the office where Mr. Thomas sat when he was in.

Mr. Figg nodded to him as he took his place behind the mahogany desk. "Mr. Kincaid," he said, then he shook his head. "No, it is Lord Ashford now, is it not?"

So they had heard. "It is, but there is no need for such formality here. I've told you for years, Figg, that you may call me Marcus."

"I prefer formality, my lord, and your title demands it now. So what is it that I can do for you today, Lord Ashford? As you probably remember, Mr. Thomas does not come in until later in the day." He opened a ledger on the desk. "Would you like me to schedule you an appointment to see him?"

Marcus took a seat near Figg's desk and looked around. On the remaining walls hung maps of all the places they currently handled tours. Marcus had led all of them save the ones to America.

"I submitted my proposed itinerary for the Around the World tour several months ago. Has Mr. Thomas not made his decision yet?" Marcus still felt certain his plans would be selected. Mr. Thomas had always favored him; he had been a leader in this place.

Mr. Figg smiled. "Mr. Thomas is still considering the plans. When he opened up the opportunity to all of the guides, he was not anticipating receiving plans from so many of you. He received no fewer than eight separate itineraries that he is considering." Mr. Figg closed the ledger and folded his hands on top of it. "I don't have to tell you, my lord, how important this tour is to Mr. Thomas. He wants to make certain he makes the best choice. But we certainly know whom he typically favors."

Marcus smiled.

"Will there be anything else?" Mr. Figg asked.

Marcus came to his feet. "I don't believe so. Mr. Thomas knows where to find me should he need me. Do tell him I stopped by."

"Most assuredly, my lord."

On the ride home Marcus entertained thoughts of how Vivian would fare on one of his tours. He would wager she would find some of the countries vastly interesting. Why he would consider such matters made no sense. He wanted to seduce the woman, not spend an eight-month holiday with her.

He knew that none of the women in his life right now would understand his dedication to his employment. Yes, he did have different responsibilities now, but he would be the one to decide how to manage the two.

Chapter Eight

Two days later she found herself out shopping for new dresses for Clarissa. Lena had gone along with them to begin collecting some dresses that would grow with her increasing waistline. Vivian was still unsure how she'd been convinced to participate in this little outing. Normally, with her clients, she would develop a plan for their particular situation, and then they would carry out said plan. There didn't involve much more than what was absolutely necessary. But it seemed she was firmly enmeshed with this family, and these two women were becoming close to being considered friends. It simultaneously made her nervous and gave her joy. It had been so very long since she'd had a friend, a true friend. She did not trust people enough.

She stood in the corner of a dressmaker's shop admiring a bolt of material while Lena chatted happily with the *modiste*. Clarissa was being measured in a dressing room, having already selected a handful of fabrics and dress options. Vivian could probably use a new dress or two, as she did enjoy staying at the height of fashion. It wasn't so much vanity as that it aided in maintaining her reputation. In London, people wouldn't trust your advice if they didn't approve of your wardrobe.

"This is it, Vivian, I have found something for you. This is the perfect color for your complexion. Come and see." Lena's cheery face beamed from the other side of the store.

Vivian made her way to where Lena held a bolt of shimmering blue material. "Gracious, Lena, but that is a bright color. Whatever would I do with a dress made in such a fabric?" She had to admit, though, that the material was stunning. It was hard to look away from, and it seemed to beckon her to reach over and run her fingers along the silky length.

"Don't be silly. Why wouldn't you have a dress made with this? You would look stunning in it." She narrowed her eyes. "Why is it that you do not like men?"

Vivian looked up from the azure material. "What does that have to—" She shook her head. "I don't believe I ever said I did not like men. But all the same, I am well past courting years and I have neither the time nor the patience to sidestep any lonely gentlemen."

Lena's brow creased. "That is poppycock! You are most certainly not past courting years. I would wager my purse of coins that you could marry anyone of your choice."

Vivian gave an unladylike snort. "Even though I know you are wrong, I am not naive enough to take that gamble. I have the sneaking suspicion you win most of your wagers."

Lena smiled. "You are correct, Vivian. But I do know one gentleman who is rather fond of you."

"Who?" Her own tone and quickness of response irritated her. Why should it matter? No man would want her if he knew the truth about her past. Men did not want spoiled goods, as it were.

"You cannot tell me you have not noticed. Marcus certainly seems quite taken with you." She brought her hand to her chest and gave a great dramatic sigh.

Vivian knew she blushed. She looked back down at the fabric in her hand, and allowed it to drop from her grasp. It fell away like blue water running through her fingers. She turned away to another rack of material. He needed to be careful if other people were beginning to notice how he looked at her.

"Marcus feels nothing more than gratitude." She fingered lavender chintz. "For helping with Clarissa," she said over her shoulder.

"Honestly, Vivian, I do not take you for a fool." Lena walked to her. She stood a good head taller than Vivian. "I've seen the way he looks at you." Her brows rose and she gave her a knowing look.

Vivian's stomach fluttered. She knew precisely what Lena meant. Vivian had seen the look of desire in Marcus's eyes, but she'd done her best to ignore it. Knowing someone else saw it too… she could not allow herself to entertain such thoughts. She had had her one indiscretion in life, and she could not afford another.

"Lena, he is a man of a certain age and he has been traveling for the better part of the last decade. I suppose he looks at all women to whom he is not related that way." She waved her hand. "It means nothing." She held up a chartreuse silk from the rack. "This is a lovely color, Lena. It would go wonderfully with your hair."

"I've seen desire on a man's face, and that is what I see when Marcus looks at you. But I shall cease pestering you about it." She picked up the bolt and held it up to her body. "You do have a point about this color. It is wonderful."

"Whatever it is you see in Marcus will no doubt disappear when he sees all the lovely young women at the balls we're taking him to."

"We shall see, I suppose. I am going to buy this material. And I'm going to get that other one for you."

Vivian frowned. "Which one?"

"The blue." Lena nodded once in confirmation.

"There is no need to purchase anything for me. I have more than enough money. Besides, I think it is far too bright for me. I tend to favor warmer colors."

"It will be good for you. You wear too many dark and drab colors. No offense, dear, but you are a lovely woman. You should wear more colors that set off your attributes." She tugged on the sleeve of Vivian's dark brown gown for emphasis.

Vivian could never take offense at Lena; she was too genuine and good-hearted. True, she spoke her mind and often said things a person did not want to hear, but Vivian knew she always meant well.

"Even so, you do not need to purchase it. I can very well pay for it myself."

"I know you can, but I also know you take no payments for—" She lowered her voice. "—the services you provide. You have done wonderful things for my family and I know in the end Clarissa's reputation will be salvaged."

She knew arguing with Lena would do no good, so she

merely nodded in concession. The fabric was stunning, but she doubted it would do much for her. Vivian knew she was not an unattractive woman, but she was hardly beautiful by today's standards. And regardless of how everyone lately kept trying to disregard the truth, she knew she was older. She was four and thirty, well past the time women prettied themselves up to garner the attention of a suitor.

It took another twenty minutes to finalize the order for Clarissa's new dresses. When it was, the three of them they returned to the street, where they stopped at a shop and purchased new ribbons and then a trinket shop where Lena bought a silver rattle for the baby.

"I just cannot wait for this little one to join us," Lena said as they left the shop.

Vivian didn't think she and Lena were that different in age, but Lena had been married for years. Evidently, she and Henry had tried a long time for this baby. It was standard for women their age to be married with children. No one ever dared ask Vivian why she was unmarried, but she knew they probably wondered. Aristocrats were a nosy bunch.

Did everyone believe her to be a bitter old spinster pining away for a love lost and a missed chance for children? There had been a time when she'd desired a family of her own, had longed for a husband to love her, and children to raise. Life had had other plans for her. Or in truth, she'd made a horrible mistake, one from which she could never recover. So now she simply did not think about such things.

"Clarissa, have you spoken with Mr. Wilbanks lately?" Vivian asked.

Clarissa smiled broadly. "I have not. He's out of town, gone to Stratford to purchase some new horses."

"And you are so certain you will marry him?" Lena asked.

"Oh yes, we are a perfect match," Clarissa said.

Vivian wanted to scream at the girl, tell her that words meant nothing, that until a man had you in front of a minister, it meant nothing. But she kept her lips tightly shut. While she was finding a bride for Marcus, she should most definitely find someone else for Clarissa before the girl found herself heartbroken and compromised.

They passed through a group of people standing outside a milliner's shop.

"Vivian March," a man's voice said.

The little hairs on her forearms stood on end. Vivian stopped walking and turned around to face the group, searched their faces. She knew that voice.

"Vivian, is everything all right?" Lena asked.

Where was he? She'd know his voice anywhere, but he was nowhere to be seen. Could she have been mistaken?

"Yes. Did you hear someone call my name?" she asked her companions.

Clarissa shook her head. "I was talking about George."

No, that wasn't it. She looked at Lena.

"I didn't hear it either, but I was walking on the other side of Clarissa." Her features warmed with concern. "Perhaps we should get you home."

Vivian nodded. "I must be more tired than I thought," she said with a smile. She took one more look at the people gathered around, but saw no sign of him. No sign of Frederick Noble, but she knew for certain she hadn't been wrong.

The bastard was back.

• • •

Vivian sat on the bench seat at the foot of her bed, fingering the material of the dress that lay across her lap. She took a deep breath and held the material up to the light. It was so brilliant she would no doubt look frightfully pale, if not ill, in it.

If she was right and Frederick was back, she would see him soon at some outing or another. He'd always loved high society—balls and soirees and the theatre. She would see him, and when she did she would have to somehow find a way to speak with him privately. It was in both their interests that their previous affair remain a secret, and she needed a moment to remind him of that. She'd already sent a note to his brother's townhouse inquiring about Frederick's return, but had received a polite note saying that as far as the family knew, he remained in France.

A small knock sounded at the door and then it opened to reveal her aunt. "I hope I'm not disturbing you, but I thought you might need some help, especially since it would seem that you sent your lady's maid scurrying away." Her head tilted and she frowned. "Why are you not dressed?"

Vivian shook her head and stood. She placed the dress on the bed. "I don't think I can go through with this. I mean, look at it. Look at me. We simply do not match."

Rose looked at the dress and then looked around the room, and peeked out into the hall. When she came back in, her eyes narrowed. "What have you done with my niece?"

"Whatever are you talking about?"

"Vivian, you are a bold and confident woman. It is

merely a dress. A beautiful dress, but you love fashion. This is simply a brighter color than you would normally wear."

"Not to mention the cut is far more revealing than I'm accustomed to," Vivian said with a snort.

"Still. You don't have nerves such as these." She sat next to Vivian and put her aging hand on top of Vivian's. "What is bothering you, my dear?"

She longed to tell her aunt everything, to start with Frederick and end with Marcus's maddening kisses that made her want things she had no right to want. But she couldn't tell her any of that. So she laughed. It was intended to sound light and airy, and instead sounded like a strained chuckle. "I'm being a ninny," she said. "I do not know what is bothering me. You are absolutely right. I do love fashion and this is a beautiful dress. I am confident and I'm going to wear it." She came to her feet before she lost that feigned confidence. "Will you help me, Aunt Rose?"

Her aunt helped her into the dress. She pulled the sleeves in place and adjusted the bodice and swished her hips to right the skirts. Vivian ran her hand up the back of her dress as far as she could reach. "How many buttons does this thing have?" she asked as she walked to the heavy mirror hanging on the wall.

Rose shook her head. "Too many. I do hope I can do this quickly enough."

Vivian stood facing the mirror as her aunt fastened each button. The more she clasped, the more the shape of the dress came into focus. The shimmery blue material scooped down in a daring décolletage. The cap sleeves were accented with feathers dyed to match the dress. A darker blue ribbon tied at her waist made her look shapelier than she would have thought. The tunic skirt split in front and was tied up with bows. The underskirt was layered with pleats, each linked with the same blue ribbon. It was unlike any dress she had ever worn, and despite her inclination otherwise, she had to admit that it looked quite magnificent on her.

"Good heavens, it shows a lot of flesh, don't you think?" She placed her hand on the skin above her breasts. "I believe I might spill out of this."

Rose laughed. "If I had a figure like yours, *I'd* wear my dresses even lower." Her eyes widened and she smiled playfully.

Vivian tapped her aunt on the arm. "You are truly awful, Aunt Rose."

"Age does something to you, dear." She shook her head wistfully. "I tell you, if I had to do it all over again, I would have lived my life differently."

"You have regrets?"

Rose chuckled. "More than I'd like to admit." She winked. "I would have lived my life with more debauchery. Enjoy yourself tonight." She kissed Vivian on the cheek and then stepped out of the room.

Had her aunt just given her permission to…no, she wouldn't even think such a thing. She closed her eyes against the reflection in the mirror.

Her maid entered the room cautiously and Vivian found herself at her dressing table. She felt the gentle poke of the hairpins as the maid secured her wild curls away from her face, and then the girl was gone. Vivian would have to make a point of apologizing to her tomorrow.

She opened her eyes. The maid had done a lovely job with her hair. Forget-me-nots decorated the upswept curls, their pretty blue color matching her dress perfectly. Something was missing, though. Vivian opened the lid to her trinket box and found the jewelry she sought—a necklace and earrings with diamonds and sapphires. She put them both in place and knew that despite the way she felt, she was ready.

Aunt Rose was right—she was confident, and she never allowed anyone to make her feel out of place. Tonight was about introducing Marcus to potential brides, but there was absolutely no reason that she couldn't wear a beautiful dress.

She met Clarissa, Aunt Maureen, Lena, and Henry outside the Wellbrook house. They entered the ballroom together. Marcus was supposed to meet them here, but so far she had not seen him.

The Wellbrook ball was always one of the best of the year. They hired the most renowned musicians and served the most delectable food and their decorations—well, only the queen herself did better. The room glittered with hundreds of candles. Gold and green brocade decorated the room, hanging from the tall windows and draping gracefully to the floor.

Vivian scanned the room. Relief flooded through her to see that her dress fit smartly with the rest of the evening's fashion. She felt quite certain that no one would even notice she wore something so different for her.

Lena waved brightly to a couple walking by while Henry nodded and spoke to everyone in their path. Clarissa quickly made her excuses and left them to go find her friends.

"Darling, do you see Marcus anywhere?" Lena asked.

"Do you suppose he's here this early? I would think the

boy would be fashionably late," Henry said.

Vivian had made up her mind she was not going to be foolish. She had been to hundreds of these events. Her nerves betrayed her. Ordinarily, she was not a believer in imbibing spirits to calm oneself, but perhaps tonight she needed some assistance, if only a small sip of champagne.

"I believe I'm going to find myself a beverage," she told her companions.

Lena put a hand on her arm to still her movements. "Henry, would you be so kind as to fetch Vivian some champagne?"

"Of course." He kissed his wife sweetly on the cheek and walked towards the refreshment table, whistling a jolly tune.

"He has such a pleasant manner about him."

"Always. When we first met," she said, scrunching up her face, "it made me absolutely insane. I refused to believe anyone could be that genuinely kind. But then I fell in love and now it is as endearing to me as his little bald head." She laughed. "Is it not amazing how love can make one blind to others' faults? Sometimes even those very things that irritate you become the little things that you love the most."

Vivian nodded, although she wasn't sure if she agreed. She had never truly loved anyone. Not in the manner Lena described. She had once fancied herself in love, but in time she had come to realize it was merely her body's desires, her own weaknesses.

She wondered what it felt like to sleep beside a man who loved her. Knowing that man's heart warmed with thoughts of only her. What did it feel like to wake with one man's name on your lips? Everything she'd experienced with love had been deception, but clearly there were happy unions like Lena's and Henry's.

"Well, if it isn't the two most beautiful women here."

Marcus's voice interrupted her thoughts, and her breath caught at the sight of him. Dressed all in black, except for the shock of white of his shirt, he was the embodiment of handsomeness.

He kissed Lena's cheek. "Good evening, my dear cousin."

"I daresay you look quite dashing. Wouldn't you agree, Vivian?" Lena asked.

Vivian met his gaze. His brows rose as if expecting her answer. "Yes, he looks quite handsome. Certainly handsome enough to grab the attention of plenty of available young women."

Henry appeared with her champagne and a lemonade for Lena. He fussed over his wife, distracting her, which gave Marcus the opportunity to take a step closer to Vivian.

"You," he said, meeting Vivian's glance, "look exquisite. That dress…" His eyes fell to her breasts swelling from the top of the bodice. "Perfect."

Vivian took more than a ladylike sip of her champagne. Her eyes watered as the sparkling liquid slid smoothly down her throat. "I believe your Aunt Maureen is making all the arrangements for the introductions this evening. You should be making the acquaintance of plenty of acceptable young women."

Marcus watched as Vivian brought the glass back to her lips. She closed her eyes and swallowed a healthy amount. Her eyes opened again and met his. Her small pink tongue darted out and licked at the droplet of liquid remaining on her lips and Marcus nearly groaned. She was beyond tempting tonight. She was a seductress.

Her breasts rose and fell with each breath, her milky skin all but sparkled beneath the shimmering blue fabric. It molded to every curve of her body, confirming everything he'd suspected about Vivian March—she had a body made for sin. It certainly begged the question of whether or not she'd be willing to play the part of hedonist for the evening.

Chapter Nine

"Marcus, old boy, why aren't you out there putting your name on all those lovely girls' dance cards?" Henry asked.

He pulled his eyes off Vivian. "I believe I am waiting on instructions." He nodded slightly to Vivian.

As if on cue, Aunt Maureen stepped up with two women in tow. Judging from their similar features, and taking into account the age difference, he'd guess mother and daughter.

"Marcus, dear, I'd like to introduce you to Lady Brentwood and her daughter, Annie."

Marcus waited for his aunt to finish extolling his virtues before he nodded to each woman. "Enchanted," he said. He barely detected the matron Brentwood's nudge of her daughter's arm so subtle was the movement.

"My lord," Annie said abruptly. "Were your travels extensive?"

Yes, this was the part where women were taught to pretend to take interest in the pursuits of the man in question. Marcus smiled. "Mostly I traveled through India and Africa."

The girl's eyes lit with interest, interest he doubted she could feign. "India? So you have seen the great cats, the tigers?"

"I have, and they are magnificent creatures, powerful and sleek. I have seen lions and leopards and panthers, as well as the tigers found in India. Hunting them for sport is a waste, if you ask me," he said knowing it was a very unpopular opinion.

Annie's hand came to her chest and she smiled broadly. "I am so glad to hear you say so. I believe the very same," she said emphatically. "My father has a—"

"That's enough, Annie, we don't want to take up all of his lordship's time. My lord," Lady Brentwood said, nodding to Marcus and then his aunt. "Maureen." And then she pulled her daughter away.

After the two women had disappeared into the crowd, Maureen turned to him. "Now then, do you see the blonde over in that group?" She nodded across from them. "You see, dear, the one in the lavender gown?"

His aunt was certainly not wasting any time, her enthusiasm indicating she'd been waiting for an opportunity such as this. Marcus followed her gaze and his eyes settled on an attractive young woman engaged in a lively conversation. She was by far the prettiest in the group. Her dress hugged her full breasts and accented her thin waist. He nodded. "She is very pretty." A fact he'd wager the lady was quite aware of, and one she no doubt used to her advantage as much as possible. He'd never found such women of much interest.

"That is Lady Constance Brindwell. Her father is a marquess. This is her second season, although I just cannot envision why that girl wasn't snatched up at her come-out during the first dance. Her mother has taken ill so her aunt is acting as her chaperone, a very dear friend of mine," she whispered behind her fan.

Vivian had been right—women did use their fans to communicate. He looked back at the group of girls and they all had fans. The accessories varied in ornamentation, and some girls held the fans while others simply allowed them to dangle from their wrists.

"She is a most lovely girl," Maureen said. "I should think you would like her very much. And see the other young lady, the taller one in the light blue dress? Not as comely, but she has the gentlest spirit. Sweet dear, that is Gwyneth Montrose. Her father is a wealthy merchant, highly respected, and hopes to find a kind man in the upper class. Why don't I introduce you to them?"

It was not a question. Aunt Maureen knew how to put things so they did not sound like a demand. She held out her arm to him and he escorted her to the group of ladies. What did it matter if he met them? This was an exercise in futility. Should he decide he wanted a wife, he would damn well pick her out himself.

"Lady Constance and Miss Montrose, I should like you to meet my nephew. He has been abroad traveling but has returned recently. May I present Marcus Kincaid, Earl of Ashford."

The pretty Lady Constance curtsied, then gave him a brilliant smile. She held out her hand and he bowed over it, and did the same with Miss Montrose. "A pleasure to meet you both."

"Indeed," Lady Constance said. Her tone and eyes

bespoke a confidence that innocent girls normally didn't possess. "My lord, I have already heard so much about you. This ballroom is positively abuzz with talk of you and your adventures."

That he seriously doubted. More than likely they were all discussing his marital status, his estates, and how much income he maintained.

"Do you travel?" he asked her.

"Of course. My family takes an annual holiday to Brighton, and I have an aunt in Northampton," Lady Constance said.

He didn't particularly consider that travel, but he would not bring that to her attention. "That must make your aunt so happy for you to visit her. I know that my lovely aunt here is very proprietary about my time. I promised her a trip to the refreshment table, so if you would excuse us…?"

He bowed slightly, nodded to the other ladies, then turned and escorted his aunt away. He started back in the direction where he had left Vivian and Lena.

"My beloved nephew, if you are to take me to the refreshment table, as promised," she said, emphasizing the last words, "then I believe we're going in the wrong direction."

He smiled sweetly at her. "Of course, we don't want to forget your lemonade."

"Now then, I do believe there are a few more girls for you to meet, but after this brief excursion, I should like to sit and rest for a while," Aunt Maureen said.

He couldn't help but wonder if Vivian had been watching him meet her bridal candidates. After they retrieved his aunt's beverage, they turned toward their party, and Marcus got his answer. Not only was Vivian not looking in his direction, she stood entranced in a conversation with another gentleman. An older gentleman, from what Marcus could tell by the gray in the man's hair.

"Who is that gentleman with our party?" he asked Aunt Maureen.

"Oh, would you look at that — that is the Earl of Banberry." Maureen clapped her hands. "He's been a widower for the last ten years. Raised his children alone. I am so pleased to see he has rejoined society. What a charming gentleman, and it does appear he has taken a liking to Miss March."

Marcus sped up their pace.

"Gracious, Marcus, remember that I am not a young girl." Although her words were stern, her face glowed with a smile.

"How did you fare with Lady Constance and Gwyneth?" Lena asked when Marcus reached their circle.

"Who?" Marcus asked absently.

Her brow furrowed. "Why, the young ladies you just met."

"Oh." Marcus shook his head. "Right. I am bad with names. They were charming." The truth was, he couldn't recall anything either of them had said.

"Splendid, well, I don't believe you've met the Earl of Banberry." Lena pulled at his sleeve to turn him around. "My lord, this is my cousin, Marcus Kincaid, the new Earl of Ashford."

Marcus plastered on his best smile and shook the man's hand. "A pleasure to meet you, Lord Banberry." The old goat was not nearly as old as Marcus had first guessed. More than likely he wasn't a day over forty, an age perhaps more to Vivian's liking.

"My very dear friend and neighbor, Lady Worthington,

remembered Miss March and was kind enough to introduce me to your party," Banberry said. "I have been out in the countryside for so long, I scarcely remember anyone. Ah, but I could never forget a gem such as yourself, Mrs. Pringle." He bent over Maureen's hand.

Maureen grinned like a schoolgirl, her cheeks stained pink.

"What brings you to the city?" Marcus asked.

"I am ready to marry again," he said matter-of-factly. "I have raised my children and now have a large home all to myself. In all truthfulness, I get bored and lonely. There are only so many times a man can ride each day. I want companionship."

"It seems we have similar agendas, Banberry. I too find myself in need of a wife." Marcus met Vivian's eyes.

"I certainly wish you the best of luck. I know how difficult it is to find the right woman. I suppose I never thought I would have to do it again."

As much as Marcus didn't want to admit it, the earl was polite and sincere. Marcus nodded in what he hoped was a cordial manner, then excused himself.

Marcus stood in the shadows watching the ballroom before him. He'd had enough. After he'd walked away from his family earlier to go in search of something stiffer to drink than champagne, his aunt had found him. She'd introduced him to a handful of additional girls and their eager mothers. It was enough to send any bachelor into hiding. But mostly he hid to watch one particular woman.

Vivian effectively worked her magic with Clarissa's predicament. She led his sister from one group to the next seamlessly, and all seemed more than welcoming to Clarissa. From his vantage point, though, he could always see someone else watching Vivian. For nearly a quarter of an hour the tall brunette had watched every move Vivian made. The woman wasn't particularly attractive, though she had a sensuality about her in the way that she scanned the room, the way she moved her body.

He'd inquired subtly about the woman and discovered her name was Diana Cosgrove. She was unmarried and as far as everyone knew, had no male attention of any sort. But she watched Vivian's every move. Marcus had begun to wonder if the tall woman was attracted to Vivian, but then he'd seen her sneer. A small movement of her lips and a glare of her eyes, but enough hatred to clearly be seen were one watching as he'd been. Diana Cosgrove loathed Vivian March. He couldn't help but wonder why. Vivian was certainly not the most gregarious woman in the room, but she was always poised and charming.

Vivian excused herself from the group she currently stood with and then walked close enough for him to grab her by the elbow. She had the good sense not to cry out at the abrupt movement and the moment she caught sight of him, she whacked him on the arm.

"Whatever did you do that for? There's no reason for us to be hiding out in this darkened hallway," Vivian said.

"I wanted a moment to speak to you."

"And you cannot do so in the ballroom?"

"No, I wanted to speak in private."

She rolled her eyes. "Well, I am here now. What is it

you wish to discuss with me? Don't tell me you've already disregarded every woman you've been introduced to."

He wouldn't tell her so, though he certainly had done precisely that for a variety of reasons. One was too tall, another too thin, yet another had an annoying, squeaking voice that grated on his ears, not unlike the mating sounds of flamingos. But he wouldn't tell her any of that. Not yet, at least. For now he'd allow her to believe she was perfectly capable of finding him a bride, though he had no desire for one. "No, I will not tell you that," he said. "I wanted to ask you about a different woman."

Her brows rose and she swallowed visibly. "You have found someone you fancy on your own?"

Was that jealousy in her tone? "No, I am merely curious as to your relationship with Diana Cosgrove."

"What are you talking about, Marcus? I have no relationship with Diana Cosgrove. I barely know the woman."

As if the woman could sense their discussion, she came near to their hiding place, too close for Marcus to feel comfortable. He gripped Vivian tighter and slipped them into a storage pantry behind them. Enough light streamed in from beneath the other door, the one that likely led into the dining room, that he was able to see Vivian.

"What the devil are you doing?" Vivian asked.

"I didn't want you to be seen in such a compromising position," he said. "She came very close to us. You could have been seen speaking with me."

"We weren't in a compromising situation, we were merely having a conversation in the hall. *Now* we are in a compromising situation." Her frustration made her breathing labored, and her breasts rising and falling above her neckline nearly drove him mad.

He pulled her tighter. "Indeed we are. Stay close so that we can speak in hushed tones." He leaned down so that his breath would feather across her ear. "Do you have any idea how delicious you look in this dress? How am I supposed to be interested in other women when you put them all to shame?"

She sucked in her breath and for a moment seemed lost in his eyes. She frowned and again popped him on the arm. "Stop that. You wanted to speak to me, now hurry on with it so I can return to the ball."

"Tell me what it is that makes Miss Diana Cosgrove glare at you in such a fashion."

She shivered at his words. "I haven't the slightest idea. We've barely spoken to one another, though we certainly share friends and acquaintances. I didn't realize she wished me ill."

Interesting. So Vivian had never noticed. It seemed unlikely tonight was the first night Diana had felt such anger. The animosity she aimed at Vivian was sharp, certainly not a mild annoyance.

"Did you hear her say something?" Vivian asked.

"No, I merely watched her watching you. Unlike the rest of London, whom you've effectively enamored, she seems unmoved by your charms."

"Perhaps she has a sour stomach." Vivian shrugged. "Honestly, I have no notion why she would dislike me so. I don't suppose everyone looks at me with such favor."

"Perhaps." But he doubted as much. The situation warranted some investigation. He leaned down and kissed Vivian's cheek lightly. "Why are you so intent on marrying me off when we have only recently been reunited?"

"Reunited? It is not as if you and I were lovers."

"No, but we could be," he said, all the while lavishing kisses down her face to her bare collarbone. God, she smelled good, like fresh berries and cream. "Consider it."

"I will do no such thing. I am not interested in becoming your lover," she said, though her voice was unconvincing. Her voice had taken on a husky tone filled with desire.

"You can't say that with certainty." He met her mouth for a tender but brief kiss, one that would leave her wanting more. "Think about that tonight as you lie in bed. If you took me as your lover, I would kiss you all over. Every last inch of your being, Vivian. I would leave no flesh untouched."

"You are a wicked man, Marcus," she murmured.

"Indeed. Won't you be a little wicked with me?"

She took a steadying breath. "Not tonight I won't." And then she slipped out of the closet.

But she hadn't said no.

• • •

Vivian had let it slip that she was taking Aunt Rose to the theatre, as was their tradition once the new Season began. Marcus then had his own aunt make arrangements for two of the young women he'd met, along with their mothers, to join him and sit in his box at the very same performance. So it was that Vivian stood in the theatre lobby knowing full well that Marcus would arrive at some point. She had to give him credit. He had said he was coming after her and he'd certainly been true to his word.

The theatre fluttered with people. Beautiful young

women and fashionable older women milled about in brightly colored dresses as if attempting to compete with the fresco paintings along the arched ceilings. Tall and stately men, dressed in their finest, stark white ties and black tails, spoke above the women, using their deep voices to fill the room with talk of politics, travel plans, and finance.

Good heavens, but there were a lot of bodies in this room! Rose finally made it away from her throng of acquaintances to Vivian's side. "Shall we take our seats?" Rose asked.

"Indeed. It seems even more congested than usual out here," Vivian said. She'd never before been bothered by crowds, but tonight they all seemed to be standing too close, talking too loudly.

Finally in their seats, Vivian held the theatre glasses up to better see all the people around them. The crowd had evidently followed their lead, and more and more people were filtering in to their seats. The boxes nearest her filled with their patrons. She wondered if Lena and Henry were here. Or if Clarissa and Maureen had come. But no matter what name flitted through her mind, her eyes sought a certain dark-haired, blue-eyed devil.

She tried to convince herself that it was simply the unknown. Once she knew where he sat, and which girls he'd invited, she would be able to relax and enjoy the performance. She knew, though, that neither of those things were true in the least.

She peered through the magnifying glasses and scanned the room. To her right, she spotted a couple having a disagreement. She could tell by the woman's thin-lipped mouth and narrowed eyes. The woman did not look at her husband. Instead, she kept her eyes coolly looking forward, while her mouth still moved.

Vivian moved on to the next area of rows. Three young and very pretty girls sat, all smiles and giggles, backs straight and dressed in the colors of sweet cakes. Vivian smiled wistfully. She remembered being that young and full of hope at the possibilities of life. She willed the girls to be strong, to not make the same mistake she'd made, so that they could go on to find love or at the very least a husband whom they did not loathe.

A box seat across from and above her housed a crush of people. An older couple, the man already sleeping and the woman chatting happily to the person in front of her. Three more middle-aged women, two younger women, both of whom seemed to be studying their programs, two men standing…and one pair of theatre glasses staring back at her. She pulled her glasses away from her eyes, but kept her sight on the box. She looked through the glasses again. This time she saw the person, and he smiled brilliantly and winked.

Caught you.

Marcus had been watching Vivian peer through her glasses for the last several moments. He hoped she'd looked for him. Her Aunt Rose sat beside her chatting happily away, despite the fact that Vivian obviously hadn't been paying attention.

Vivian looked beautiful, though he noted she'd gone back to her normally favored dark colors with a deep green gown. Again, she lifted her glasses and looked his way. Her mouth opened and she quickly removed the glasses and looked away. Marcus chuckled.

It was perfect that she knew where he was sitting. She could easily see he was following their bargain of bride hunting, as he'd invited two of the women to join him this evening.

Lady Constance looked beautiful in an icy blue gown. It set off her fair complexion and pale blonde hair. Though she was an attractive woman, there was something about her that Marcus didn't care for. He hadn't selected the women for this evening's gathering. He'd left that to his aunt, and evidently she was encouraging that particular alliance since she was rather fond of Constance's aunt. The two elder women now sat gossiping contentedly.

It was a study in contrast between Lady Constance and the other woman invited, Annie. Constance stood a good head above petite Annie. With her darker complexion, from her French mother, he'd been told, and hair nearly black, Annie was the very opposite of Lady Constance's golden beauty. He would marry neither, though he found Annie's pleasant nature far more appealing than Constance's seductive glances.

As soon as the lights dimmed, Lady Constance moved from her seat to the empty one next to him. "Have you ever seen this play, my lord?"

He leaned a little closer so she could hear his lowered voice. "I don't believe I have. My travels have not allowed for many visits to the theatre. And yourself?"

"No, not this one. But I adore the theatre. The stories they weave." She leaned even closer. "May I tell you a secret?"

What kind of secret could a young woman of nineteen

or twenty have? No doubt as dreadful as "my slippers are not the precise color of my gown."

Her eyes dropped to his mouth and she leaned even closer. "It is a wicked secret," she whispered. "Not one for a proper lady." She paused only a second. "I have a fantasy of being on stage, of being the center of the room with all eyes watching. Listening only to me. Thinking only of me."

She was a brazen one, he would admit that. With her pouty, kiss-me lips and wide blue eyes, she appeared innocent, but her words and movements spoke of a worldly experience not learned from books. At one point in his life, her charms and obvious sexuality would have sent his desire over the edge. Tonight he felt nothing. Well, not exactly nothing. If the truth be told, he felt a little unsettled.

The curtains opened and the play began.

Marcus raised his glasses and found Vivian. She appeared enchanted by the actors on the stage and even laughed at some of their antics.

Marcus saw very little of the play. Instead, he kept his attention divided between watching Vivian and trying to pretend he was interested in the play. Vivian's face lit with laughter and Marcus would have given anything to be sitting at her side to hear the giggle. That was not about seduction, though. Seduction was about moans and sighs of pleasure. Giggles were an entirely different matter, one he wasn't so certain he was comfortable with.

Chapter Ten

Vivian was nearly thankful that the morning after the theatre, she awakened to find a distraught Lady Milford in her front parlor. It was a small issue that required little creativity to work out. Still, dealing with the woman's mother-in-law, who insisted on making very public wagers on nearly everything with anyone who would approach her, was far more appealing to think upon than the current mess in Vivian's own life. Once that issue was resolved, Vivian had to turn her thoughts once again to the Kincaid family.

After she'd seen him at the theatre, and the mere thought of him had set her heart to racing, Vivian had nearly considered retiring to the country for the remainder of the Season. Then on her way home, her aunt had told her that people were still discussing Clarissa's indecorous meeting with Justin Rodale. Evidently, it was going to be a more trying rumor to squelch, and his welcome presence in society hadn't yet helped. Every now and again those types of scandals popped up, like sparks blowing in the wind that started one fire here, another over there.

So it became evident that she could not walk away, not yet. The sooner Marcus became engaged, the sooner people would forget about Clarissa, and the sooner Vivian could forget about Marcus. Luckily, they had all agreed to attend the Finches' ball that evening. It was time for him to begin courting those women and make a selection.

Later that evening at the Finches' ball, Vivian shook her head at what Marcus had just said. He thought his request had been completely legitimate, but she evidently disagreed. She grabbed his sleeve and pulled him to a corner heavily guarded by an alarmingly large potted topiary.

Two girls walked by them, their arms linked and they whispered, never even looking up to see Marcus and Vivian.

"Your impertinence is truly becoming tedious," Vivian said.

A footman stopped to offer them champagne. Vivian shot the man in impatient look. "Not now, thank you," she said tartly. She turned back to Marcus. "Why must you be so damned stubborn?"

Marcus put his hand to his chest. "Why, Miss March, such indecorous language coming from you. And at the Finches' ball. It's truly scandalous."

"I am serious." And she was, of that he was certain. Her brow furrowed and little lines had formed at the edges of her eyes. Her stance, too, spoke of a woman quite incensed.

"I am, too. *Those* are my terms. Accept them or not, it

matters not to me." He shrugged.

She crossed her arms over her ample bosom and glared at him. "And if I do not wish to dance with you?" she asked.

"Then I shall not dance at all." He smiled at her. "It's really quite simple, Vivian."

"There is nothing about you that is simple. Absolutely nothing." She exhaled loudly. "*You* are an infuriating man."

"And yet you still find me attractive." He ran one finger down the part of her arm exposed between her sleeve and glove.

She shivered against his touch, but said nothing, merely continued to glare.

"One dance, Vivian, that is all. Certainly you can stand to be in my arms for the length of one waltz."

Another footman came back, this time offering lemonade, and Marcus held up one hand. The man walked off without saying a word.

"Another dance. Any dance but the waltz," she said. Her brown eyes met his and he almost agreed. But the fact was he didn't want to dance with any of those women. If he had to dance, he wanted her in his arms and the waltz was the only way to get her close to him.

"No, it must be the waltz."

"Damnation, Marcus, do you not realize that people are still talking about your sister? The rumor has not died. Her reputation is still at risk."

"Then convince her to marry someone. That would save her reputation," Marcus said. "She will not listen to me."

Vivian shook her head. "It will not work. She's convinced herself that she is to marry George Wilbanks, though it's becoming abundantly clear he has no intention of marrying her." Then Vivian frowned. "You don't think—"

"No, they're never alone. Maureen guards her particularly closely. Especially now," Marcus said. "And I'm not so certain George is all that interested in Clarissa, at least not romantically. They have been friends for years, though. And I've already spoken to her about him. She has been given explicit instructions not to spend any more time with Wilbanks. If he does want to marry her, let him come speak to me about it formally."

"Well, I must say I find your stance on that quite admirable," she said.

"See, I've already impressed you for the evening. Reward me with a dance."

"Forbidding her to see George Wilbanks is a good start, but you should also be encouraging her to select another man that might be a better choice for her."

He did want Clarissa to marry—that was in his best interest, would allow him to return to his employment sooner—but he would not force the girl into a marriage that would make her miserable. "I will consider speaking to her."

"So knowing full well your sister's good name is in potential danger, you still will not do what is necessary to save her?" Vivian asked.

"It sounds to me as if you are the one not doing what is necessary. You were the one brought in as the expert in this particular situation. You should be more creative. Marrying me off can't be the only solution to this problem." He gripped her arm, and wanted very badly to pull her closer to him. "Besides, why should I have to saddle myself for a lifetime with some woman I do not know to make up for an innocent conversation my sister had?" He smiled at her, the grin a woman had told him once made it impossible to resist him. "Vivian, would it be so awful to dance with me? One waltz and I shall dance with whomever you wish me to tonight."

"You are making a scene," she said. She pulled herself out of his grip.

"Seems the smart thing to do would be to dance with him," Justin said as he walked past them.

Vivian frowned at Justin's back, and then she met Marcus's gaze.

"I could not have planned that if that's what you're wondering," Marcus said. "You are the one who pulled me over here, I might remind you. We have been here for a while. I suspect people could start talking about us."

"I have no interest in dancing with you."

"Love, you are far too angry for me to believe that. Do save me that waltz."

"Insufferable," she muttered before she stalked off.

"Why are you tormenting her so?" Justin asked when Marcus walked up to him. "Poor Miss March."

Why was he tormenting her? Because ever since he'd kissed her again, he'd thought of little else but when he could get her back into his arms. He wanted to lay her bare and spend hours exploring every glorious part of her body. "I do not wish to be married."

"No one is going to require you to marry," Justin said. "She merely wanted you to dance with them." He glanced at the room around them. "Do you realize I know the size of the purse of nearly every man in this room?"

Marcus chuckled. "I suppose your presence makes quite a few of them rather nervous."

"Ah yes, I inadvertently scowled at Lord Archer at the

refreshment table and I believe he scurried away crying."
Justin swirled the amber-colored drink in his glass.

"How much is he in for?"

"Seven hundred pounds, at last check." Justin sipped his
drink. "So you intend to marry Miss March?"

"No, marriage is not really in my mind at the moment."

"You are a rake of the worst sort, then. Seducing an
innocent woman." Justin's words held no judgment. But
they also held no truth. Vivian March was no innocent and
Marcus had every intention of enjoying that to its fullest.

If Vivian had any sense at all, she'd leave now. But as she
watched Marcus dance with Gwyneth Montrose, Vivian
knew if she left he would make her regret it. Not only that,
if Marcus's assumption had been correct and people were
beginning to watch and discuss she and Marcus, then she had
lost control of the situation. A very worrisome conclusion.
She never lost control.

At least she hadn't until Marcus had shown up in her
life. She'd been the very pinnacle of propriety until then.
Well, except for her indiscretions with Frederick, but that
was her secret. No one else knew. No one but Frederick.

But for the moment, she needed to regain control of
this situation. Marcus Kincaid was devilishly handsome
and for whatever reason, he seemed to enjoy ruffling her
feathers. And she, whatever the reason, allowed him to do
so. He certainly wasn't the first man to flirt with her. Though,
admittedly, he was the first to steal such searing kisses from
her.

He caught her glance from the dance floor and she could have sworn he winked. She looked behind her to see if anyone else had seen his brazenness, but a group of people behind her were discussing politics. How could people discuss politics at a time such as this? She was going to have to dance with that man in front of everyone. She took a steadying breath. She rarely danced.

"He is very handsome," a woman's voice said beside her.

Vivian turned and saw Diana Cosgrove standing at her side. Marcus had only just inquired about Miss Cosgrove the other day and now she was speaking to Vivian for the first time. "I beg your pardon?"

"Lord Ashford. I have not made his acquaintance as yet, but he is quite dashing," Diana said.

She was an attractive woman, but not one you would consider beautiful. With her red hair and lazy green eyes she stared out across the ballroom at Marcus. The way she watched him made Vivian uncomfortable. Yes, he was on the market for a wife, but Diana was close to Vivian's age and she had no business setting her sights on Marcus. "I don't believe I've had the pleasure," Vivian said, eyeing the woman. She was taller than Vivian and exuded a worldly quality.

Diana looked down, her features pinched in annoyance. "Diana Cosgrove, and I certainly know who you are. Your reputation precedes you, Miss March."

Vivian could see that was not a compliment. Evidently, Marcus had been right. For whatever reason, this woman did not think kindly of her.

"Lord Ashford is rather young for you, wouldn't you agree?" she asked, her voice taking on a feigned innocent tone.

"What is it that you have to say to me, Miss Cosgrove?" There was no reason to pretend niceties if this woman meant her harm.

Diana's delicate shoulders rose in a shrug. "Nothing more than that a mutual friend of ours asked that I bid you good evening and say that he would be seeing you soon." With that, the woman walked away.

It was a strange message, but Vivian knew precisely whom it was from. Why was Frederick playing these games? Why did he not come himself and get this over with? He was a cruel man to toy with her in such a way. She took a steadying breath. She could manage this. She was no simpering schoolgirl. There was no reason his presence should make her uncomfortable. As Miss Cosgrove said herself, Vivian had an impeccable reputation. She was Vivian March, The Paragon.

The waltz, *hers and Marcus's,* was next. The final notes to the song ended, and she knew he would be coming to retrieve her. Marcus Kincaid might believe he had the upper hand, but she knew better. She was a determined and focused woman. Frederick's return was unsettling, she couldn't deny that, but at the moment she had more pressing matters. Namely, marrying off a certain earl before he had any additional opportunities to seduce her. Once she set her mind to something, no one would dissuade her.

She sent gratitude heavenward that she wore her nicest gloves else Marcus would know her palms were sweating. The mere thought of having his hands on her body for all in the room to see had her heart thumping wildly. She had not felt so nervous dancing with Lord Banberry the other evening. She could do this. She could dance with him and no one in the room would know the truth about her. She'd hid her secret for this long, and could continue to do so.

Perhaps Marcus didn't even know the truth yet. He knew he could kiss her and get her to kiss him in return, but he was a very skilled kisser. She suspected he could do the same with any other woman in the room. He didn't know that those kisses sent wanton thoughts and images racing through her mind, making her body ache and tingle for him, making her want to press herself against him, rub herself against him in a most disgraceful sort of way. She'd kept her base urges dormant for so long he had awakened them. But this was merely a dance.

"Miss March," he said, suddenly appearing in front of her. He held out his hand to her, his perfectly masculine and ungloved hand. Her breath caught. "This is our dance."

She took another breath and met his eyes. The blue seemed to melt through her, firing desire through her every muscle. She held firm. "Yes, it is." She even managed a smile.

He took her in his arms, one hand on her back and the other holding her hand. He didn't press her body against his, but held her at an appropriate distance.

"What did Miss Cosgrove have to say to you?" he asked.

He'd been watching her; she should have known he would notice her short conversation with Diana. "Nothing, really, she introduced herself is all."

"That was it?"

"Yes, she only stopped by for a moment."

"Yes, but you seem nervous. Vivian." When she didn't immediately meet his gaze he repeated her name. "Vivian. Look at me."

She looked up again and was caught in the fathomless

depths of his azure gaze. "No, not nervous, pensive."

"It's only a dance, love," he said, his words gentle. "There is no need to fret. I merely wanted to be able to have one dance this evening where I could enjoy myself."

The words hit their mark and she nearly dissolved into a puddle of tears. How was it that this man had been in London for less than a fortnight and yet he already seemed to be able to see so much about her? See into her soul, know precisely what to say to soothe her worries. She released a heavy breath and allowed herself to take note of the music. He was an expert dancer, something she hadn't been expecting. He was graceful and fluid, and they fit remarkably well together. She lost herself in the dance, even remembered that once upon a time she'd loved dancing, in particular the waltz. He spun her around the dance floor, keeping perfect time to the music.

"You are beautiful," he said.

"There is no need for that," she said.

"No need for compliments. It was my understanding that women enjoyed it when men found them attractive."

"Women who are being courted. I am an advisor for your family in a time of need."

"You are still beautiful. My beautiful advisor."

She laughed in spite of herself. "You have a gifted tongue, but flattery will get you nowhere with me." But she felt his words. Every time he said those words, she prayed he meant them. She prayed that it wasn't merely his charm attempting to distract her, but that it was an honest sentiment that he believed her pretty.

• • •

Two nights later at the Mercer girl's coming-out ball that had promised to be the event of the Season, Vivian stood to the side watching the first of the dancers step onto the ballroom floor. She was partially hidden from much of the room by the three potted trees, but she liked it that way. Marcus had already insisted they dance; she did not want to find out what he had planned for her tonight. She had considered staying at home, but she did want to be here in case Clarissa might need her, though it did seem the girl was doing quite well.

A footman approached her with a tray. He handed her a folded piece of parchment and bowed. "A message for you, Miss March."

"Thank you," she said. She opened the paper and read the short note.

I am watching you.

Vivian looked around her, but everyone was busy dancing or conversing or standing at the refreshment table. No one that she could immediately see was looking at her. She looked to see if she could find the footman and she saw the back of his jacket heading toward a doorway, so she hurried after him. She caught up with him in a darkened corridor.

"Pardon me, sir, but who gave this to you?"

"I am not certain," he said. "I could not see his face, he only said it was imperative that you receive the message immediately."

Vivian nodded. "Thank you."

He turned and walked away.

She made a move to turn and follow him back into the ballroom, but something shifted behind her.

"Don't turn around, Vivian," a whispered voice said

from behind her.

But Vivian never had been very good at taking instructions so she turned around anyway. She could see no one, merely the shadow of someone standing in the darkened corner. "Show yourself," she said.

"It is not time. But I wanted to see you, up close." His words came out in hisses as he whispered.

She tried to listen to the voice, to see if it was Frederick's, but in such a hushed tone, it was too difficult to make out. And she didn't want to call him Frederick lest it be someone else and it created too many questions. She took a step forward. "What do you want?"

"I don't believe you're in a position to be asking questions."

She took a step toward the voice, willing her eyes to make sense of the shadow in the darkness. But none of the features would come clear.

"You'll be hearing from me soon," he said, then slipped through the door behind him.

It had to have been Frederick. Why was he playing such games with her? And why would he try to frighten her? She needed to think, and she would never be able to concentrate here at the ball. Perhaps it was time to retire for the evening. She quietly made her way back to the front of the house and called for her carriage.

Once inside, she breathed deeply to soothe her addled nerves. She should think of this logically. If one of her clients had brought this situation to her attention, seeking her guidance, what would she tell them?

Well, one thing to consider was the fact that if he had wanted to hurt her, physically speaking, he had the opportunity to do so and hadn't. So it was safe to assume that wasn't his intention. Therefore, there was no need to be frightened. She shook herself for good measure.

No, he was after something else. She recognized that his return threatened her very livelihood. Should he come forward with their story, there were many prominent families who would scorn her right out of London.

Chapter Eleven

Marcus circled the ballroom for the fourth time. This was the party Vivian had agreed upon with both Maureen and Clarissa. They'd both assured him of it when he'd asked them separately not twenty minutes before.

He'd been in the ballroom for nearly an hour and he had yet to see any sign of Vivian. He was beginning to believe she'd not come simply to avoid him. It was an annoying prospect, considering she had been the one who had set all these marriage-minded mamas in his direction. They were relentless. He'd already had to dance with three women and he'd had to be introduced to an additional four more "delightful" girls. He was finished, at least for tonight. He spotted his Aunt Maureen again and made his way over to her.

"I am leaving. Shall I take you and Clarissa home, or would you prefer I leave the carriage here for the two of you to return at your leisure?"

Maureen eyed Clarissa dancing in the center of the ballroom. "I think we'll stay. She does appear to be having an enjoyable time. And it's been a while for her."

Marcus nodded. "Very well, I'll hire a hack, and leave the carriage here for you."

She grabbed his forearm. "Are you ill?" she asked, concern etched in her features.

"No, I merely have a matter I need to attend to before retiring for the evening. All is well," he said with a pat of her hand.

Maureen nodded and he turned on his heel and left. He probably should find the hostess and give her his regards before slipping out, but he wasn't in the mood for niceties. It was one thing for Vivian to insist upon his dancing with other females, but for her to not even be there to give him something in the evening to enjoy? He would not abide that. He hired a hack and headed for Miss March's townhouse.

It was far too late for him to knock on the front door and demand to see her. He crept around to the back of the house, and could see candles burning brightly in the room he knew to be hers, and as luck would have it, there was a rather tall and strong oak tree beneath her window.

He climbed up and swung his legs over the railing of the balcony and pushed his body over the ledge. He landed with a thud, far louder than he intended and certainly loud enough to alert the woman behind the window to his presence.

True to form, Vivian swung open the French doors that led out onto the balcony. The curtains billowed in the wind. "Good heavens, Marcus, what the devil are you doing up here?" She grabbed his arm and pulled him into her room with great force, then shut the doors behind them. "Someone could have seen you."

"No one saw me," he said.

"You don't know that." She clutched the fabric at her throat closer to her body. It was not an overly revealing bit of nightwear, but the thought that it was the only thing between him and her warm, soft skin had his blood boiling through his veins. Damn, she was attractive. Her long chestnut hair had been done in one long plait that sat on her right shoulder, heavy and asking for him to reach over and touch it. Her face had been freshly scrubbed and was pink from her efforts and she smelled of lemons or oranges. Exotic and tangy.

"You haven't answered my question," she said.

"What was that?"

She frowned. "Why are you here?"

"I came to see you," he said.

"I gathered that much, but why?"

"Are you ill?" he asked.

"Heavens no. I haven't been ill a day in my life. I have a rather strong constitution."

"Then where the hell were you tonight?" He took a step towards her.

"I left early." She shrugged, crossing her arms over her chest. "Besides, I don't see any reason why I must attend every function you attend."

"Yes, but you assured us you would be there. Clarissa and Maureen were concerned." Not a complete truth, but it wasn't a huge stretch.

"Did you dance with anyone?" Vivian asked.

"Three, but only until I realized you weren't there and

weren't likely coming. That and their mamas are relentless."

"Let me guess. Annie Liddle, Gwyneth Montrose and Eloise Jennings?"

"Yes!" He rubbed at the back of his neck. "It's really quite fortunate I made it out of the ballroom alive."

"Yes, their mothers have that reputation."

He shook his head. "Vivian, why must we play this game?" He took a step toward her and grabbed her by the waist. The feel of her body without the constraints of a corset was nearly his undoing. She was soft and deliciously curvy in all the ways a woman should be. He gripped her hip as he pulled her to him. "I know you desire me."

"That has no bearing on anything."

"I want you. Does that not matter?"

"Why? Marcus, why do you want me?" she asked softly.

"I've asked myself the same question a hundred times. There is the obvious—your beauty. You are a very attractive woman. But there is so much more. For one, you have your own opinions. You do not simply repeat my words as if that were supposed to impress me. You challenge me. Mostly, though, it's this thing between us that I can't seem to explain." He ran the back of his hand down her arm. "Your effect on me, it is something I cannot walk away from until I completely explore it."

"You are imagining such things."

"Why will you not admit that you want me, too?"

"I will do no such thing." Vivian hugged her arms tighter to her chest.

"But I know that you do. I can see it in your eyes, and I certainly feel it in your kiss." He leaned close as if to kiss her, but barely brushed her jawline with his lips. He wanted to hear her say it.

"There will be no kissing," she said, her voice full of breath and desire. Despite her words, there was no defiance in her tone, no certainty of what she said.

He could lean in right now and steal a kiss, but he wanted it to go slower, wanted her to realize she wanted him, that there was in fact something heated and explosive between them.

He grabbed her wrists and pried her arms away from her body. Her nightdress was not too revealing. In all honesty, he couldn't see anything beneath the voile, but he knew she was under there. Knew that nothing but this white fabric separated him from her glorious flesh. He watched her take in breaths, watched the rise and fall of her plump breasts, and he had to fight the urge to reach up and cup them, to weigh them in his hands and feel her nipples harden at his touch.

She closed her eyes. "What are you doing?" she asked quietly.

"I can't see you, Vivian. Your gown covers everything, so there is no need to be concerned."

Her eyes snapped open. "Oh." She shook her head. "Still, you are here, in my bedroom while I'm dressed inappropriately. Well, clearly not inappropriately for my bedchamber, but with you here. Oh, this is all very improper."

He had to smile. She was normally so in control of every situation, but when she was ruffled she chattered. "We are adults," he said. "No one has to know I was here, if you're so concerned with that. But you know, Vivian, you are old enough to take a lover if you choose, and no one would say anything to you."

"I do not require a lover."

"I believe you do." He rubbed his hands up and down her bare arms. "You are so passionate. Not all women are like that, you know, but you awaken when I get near you. I feel it, I can see it in your eyes. God, it's intoxicating." He could wait no longer and he pulled her to him, felt her breasts press against his chest and cursed himself for wearing clothes. He kissed her and she kissed him right back, gave everything of herself in that kiss, opened to him and matched his need. Kissing her made him feel as if he'd never need to kiss another woman—a thought that should have given him pause, but instead it only seemed to fuel his desire.

Their kiss deepened and her hands clutched at his shoulders. She moaned into his mouth and he pressed his erection against her belly.

He wouldn't seduce her, not tonight. As much as he wanted Vivian, he knew she was more fragile than she let people know. Someone had hurt her and hurt her deeply. So despite the fact that he knew he could lay her down on that bed of hers and spend the next four hours loving every inch of her body, he forced himself to end the kiss.

He kept his forehead leaning against hers and listened to her erratic breathing. "I want you," he said, "but not tonight, not like this. When I take you—and make no mistake about it, Vivian, I will have you, under me, over me, every way I can have you—I want you to be the one to ask me." He kissed her gently on the lips and then returned to her window and left the way he'd come.

Vivian didn't dare go the window and watch him. She stood precisely where he'd left her, desire still shaking her limbs. What the devil was the matter with her?

Granted, she'd still been reeling a bit from the odd meeting at the ball earlier that night. And as soon as Marcus had arrived, she'd wanted to crumble in his arms, tell him of all the signs that pointed to Frederick's return. But then she'd have to tell him the truth about Frederick.

Had Marcus pressed the issue, gone in for a full seduction, she would not even have pretended to say no. She'd wanted him, wanted him to keep kissing her, start touching her, give her a reason to toss caution and nearly a decade of principles out the window and allow him to make love to her. And damnation if hadn't known that. He'd said as much. He would have her and she would ask him to make love to her. For a moment she'd believed him. Right now she had zero resolve. Thankfully, though, he had left and she would have time to rebuild said resolve.

She would not ask him. She couldn't. She wouldn't dare. She'd spent too much of her life denying those unladylike urges, squelching her desires and needs. Frederick had awakened that in her and she feared that if she let it loose, she'd never go back. She'd become a wanton, an immoral woman living at the edge of society where she sated her need with every willing fellow she could find. She squeezed her eyes shut against the very thought of such a thing.

She'd worked very hard to turn away from that potential disaster, focus her life on helping others, and keep her hands busy so that she didn't notice that when it came down to it, her heart was empty and lonely, and the pain of that threatened to choke the life from her.

Marcus had called her on everything. He knew she was passionate, knew her filthy little secret she'd desperately tried to hide. Did others know, too? Could they see it on her when she walked into a room? Was her weakness so obvious that men could detect it in her? She'd been flirted with before, but most of the men in London knew she wasn't interested. They knew she wasn't open for courtship, and they hadn't pursued anything else, yet Marcus had seen something in her. Perhaps it was that first kiss they'd shared so many years before. It had been a good kiss, but nothing such as the ones they'd shared since then, so it couldn't have been the memory of that all these years. No, he could see her, really see her. It was terrifying.

A part of her argued that an affair with him would solve everything, allow her to fulfill her carnal needs, perhaps permanently, so she need not feel imprisoned by them any longer. But what if that didn't happen? What if, instead, it awakened an insatiable creature inside her? What would people think? He'd said that no one would say a word if she took a lover, but she wasn't so certain. Everything she'd worked for all these years hinged on her reputation. Not only that, but every person, every family she'd assisted, they survived on her reputation as well. So it wouldn't simply be herself she was potentially damaging, but others as well. It was far too risky.

As much as she loved the thought of going to him and asking him for a heated night of passion, she couldn't afford to be that selfish, that indulgent. She had so many other people to consider, one of whom was his sister.

No matter how much she wanted to, she could not have an affair with Marcus.

"I simply cannot abide the situation here in London any longer," Vivian blurted out at breakfast the following morning.

"Your most recent project is affecting me. The man, in particular," Aunt Rose said. She set her fork down and looked up from her plate for food.

"He is incorrigible." Vivian absently smeared butter on a piece of bread. "And a rogue." Not only that, but she wanted to disappear a little while so that Frederick could not reach her.

"I have watched you, dear, as you have done this—this work of yours helping families and manipulating situations to make life's little scandals disappear into the background. You are good at it, no matter how unconventional a profession it may be. But this," she said, tapping on the table, "is different. You are more invested, more focused. This man, he is different."

Vivian shook her head. This wasn't about Marcus being different, it was that he reminded her of how different she was than most of the women she knew. With her *projects*, as her aunt was fond of calling them, Vivian had dealt with more than one young girl being compromised, losing her virtue, what have you. It was not as if she was alone in her indiscretion, but what made her so different was that she seemed incapable of turning off the urges, at least on any permanent basis. And damned if he didn't pose constant temptation to her attempts to fight those baser desires.

"My dedication to this family's plight is not unusual.

Perhaps my solution to their problem is a bit unorthodox, as I do not normally play the matchmaker, but that does not make *him* different." Vivian wrapped her arms around her chest. "He does, however, seem quite intent on driving me to Bedlam. He's not taking into consideration that all I am doing is trying to make certain that his sister's reputation is not harmed beyond repair." Vivian covered the buttered bread with a healthy dose of fig preserves.

"Are you certain that's all you're doing?" Aunt Rose asked.

"What are you implying?"

Aunt Rose shrugged. "Merely that Clarissa's reputation seems relatively unscathed, despite the fact that people are still talking about it in some circles. It appears you handled the worst of that situation already. Inviting Mr. Rodale into polite society seems to have been all the solution required. Yes, his presence makes people uncomfortable, the women are all enchanted by his dashing looks, and the men don't want him to tell anyone how much of their fortunes they've lost at his tables. And no one will go against you, dear. You've deemed him one of us and no one will argue. Clarissa will come out of this perfectly well, perhaps a little wiser, which certainly never hurt anyone."

"I want to make absolutely certain," Vivian said. "You've just said yourself that the rumors are still alive." But Aunt Rose's words tickled at her mind. If Clarissa's situation had been managed, what *was* she still doing with the Kincaid family? She desired Marcus, she knew that much, but that was her own weakness. And it seemed unlikely it was only he, but rather that he had been the first man to kiss her since Frederick. Certainly, it could have happened much sooner had another man been brazen enough to attempt to seduce her. The truth was quite clear—she was destined to be a fallen woman, and being near Marcus threatened everything she'd worked for these last nine years. She couldn't allow him to destroy that, especially with just the whisper of tender words. She challenged him. What did that even mean?

"Do you care for him?" Aunt Rose asked gently.

Vivian bristled and wanted to scream against the question. It was ridiculous, but her reaction gave her pause. Why so defensive about the matter? "Perhaps. I don't know. He confuses me. Reminds me of things I used to want, things I used to believe I could have." She turned her head away lest she show her aunt the traitorous tears in her eyes. She pretended to stare out the windows that lined the dining room, overlooking the back garden. "I am not a girl any longer."

"No, you are not, but you are not an old woman either." Suddenly her aunt was by her side, placing a warm hand on Vivian's shoulder. "Don't ignore life when it stands at your door and beckons, my sweet girl." She gave Vivian a reassuring squeeze. "I did that, more than I care to admit, while I waited for something, some perfect scenario that never came to be. And I ended up with nothing," Rose said wistfully.

She wanted to turn and comfort her aunt, tell her that her words weren't true, but by the time she'd mustered up the courage and the right words, her aunt had left the room.

She'd never before heard Rose speak of her past in such terms. As far as Vivian had ever known, both of her aunts had been maiden—or spinsters, as everyone was wont to call them—by choice. Evidently, that had not been the case, at least for Rose. But this situation with Marcus was quite different, Vivian felt certain of that. Her aunt would most assuredly not encourage her niece to have an illicit affair with a man simply because his kisses made her forget her name.

Vivian couldn't afford to care about Marcus Kincaid. She'd had her heart broken by a man once, a man with charming words and sweet seduction, and it had nearly destroyed her. She had vowed she'd never be that weak again. If she wanted a relationship with Marcus, if she decided she could manage the carnal side of herself, then she would do so on her terms. But in the meantime, it seemed he would not behave himself here in London.

She'd already called in a favor. The Dowager Duchess of Pendrake was hosting a country house party and inviting all the lovely young women Vivian had selected for Marcus. They'd have his complete attention. And, of course, Vivian could watch nearby whilst she sat with the older women and supervised the entire affair.

There was nothing that could go wrong. It was a perfect plan.

Chapter Twelve

Marcus had received the invitation and had gone immediately to Vivian's house to see what was what. She had confirmed that yes, there was to be a country house party and wouldn't it be so lovely to be able to get to know those women a little better in a quieter setting.

"You are coming, though, yes?" Marcus asked.

"Yes, of course. The dowager duchess is a dear friend of mine," Vivian said. "We went to school together, though only a year as she's older than me. Still we became dear friends in that short amount of time and have always kept in touch…"

Marcus laid himself back on the settee, stacking his boots on the sloping arm of the furniture. "I do not need to know them. They are all silly, foolish girls and I'm not interested in saddling myself with them for all eternity."

"Well, I am not of the opinion that you should marry all of them. I believe that is illegal in Great Britain," she said with a grin.

He turned his head and looked at her. "You are hilarious. That's not what I want, marrying one or all of them, in case my wants matter at all to you."

Vivian smiled at him. "Of course your wants matter. What is it that you would like to have in a wife? If you tell me, I can most assuredly find the appropriate girl for you. I'm adept at this sort of thing."

He sat up, braced his elbows on his knees, and eyed her. He had a mind to tease her, to flirt with her and toy with her, but at the end of the day that would solve nothing. It had become abundantly clear that he would, in fact, need to marry at some point. He was an earl now, the head of his family, and he would need to provide an heir lest their family fall to ruin. He couldn't allow that to happen to Clarissa or his aunt Maureen. "I haven't ever given it much thought, in all truthfulness," he said.

"You've never considered what you'd want in a partner?" she asked.

"Well, evidently you have. Why don't you tell me what you envision, and then I'll go," he said.

She waved her hand. "I am not getting married. I am a spinster."

"That's not what I asked you. You've obviously spent some time thinking about what you'd want in a husband. I'd like to know what those qualities are." He shrugged. If he knew one thing about Vivian, it was that she truly desired to help people. "It might help me get a clearer picture of what I'm looking for," he said.

She paused a moment before answering. "When I was a girl I thought of these things, but reality and fantasy are quite different." She smiled wistfully. "I always wanted a kind husband, a man who loved me dearly, someone with whom I had a great many things in common. Someone I could stay up with talking about all of life's many wonders, someone who would make me laugh, who would know how I liked my tea, someone who would buy me warm woolen stockings in the cold winter months and who would read to me from my favorite novels." She tilted her head.

She fell quiet and it was as if she had forgotten he was in the room, as if she, for a moment, had fallen into her own fantasy. She met his gaze and her eyes widened in surprise. Clearly, she had said more than she'd intended.

"Yes, well, that is why I do not spend time on such thoughts. Silly nonsense, that is," she said, the starch returning to her voice. "People don't marry for reasons such as those. Marriage is often nothing more than a business transaction, and if you're lucky, you end up with someone who might make you happy."

He'd asked to remove the pressure from himself, to jest with her a little, but in a moment of unflinching honesty, she'd made herself feel vulnerable. Now Marcus realized with great clarity that simply because he'd never before considered such things, it did not mean they wouldn't be nice to have. Her description sounded spot on. Case in point, he would have loved to have had someone to share his routing plans with when he'd been mapping out the Around the World trip. He'd worked tirelessly to come up with every element of that tour and he would wager that Vivian would have found the entire process interesting.

"I'm certainly not one who necessarily believes you must marry for love, but I have seen such unions," he said. "My brother had one. The problem isn't so much finding a love match, but keeping one. Losing his wife nearly killed Charles, he adored Rebecca so much." Marcus shifted in his seat, crossing one leg over the other. "You know, I asked him once, if it had all been worth it, if he'd do it again knowing he'd lose her anyway." He shook his head with the memory of that conversation, as fresh as if they'd had it yesterday instead of ten years before. "And Charles had responded that loving Rebecca had made him a better man and that receiving her love had been his greatest gift." Charles had gone on to say that life always came with moments of darkness and if you did not have love in your life, the darkness could swallow you whole.

And suddenly it was Marcus who had revealed too much. He'd only meant to comment on what she'd said about a love match.

Marcus eyed Vivian, trying to think of something to say, but words failed him. He grabbed her hand. "Vivian, I—" He wanted to tell her that she could still have those things, that wanting them wasn't at all foolish. The parlor door opened, saving Marcus from saying anything that would make him a greater fool than he already was.

"Miss March, you have guests," the butler said as he entered the parlor.

She pulled her hands from his and came to her feet. "Who?"

"Lord Pettyfield and his family. They said it's an emergency," the butler said.

"Very well." Vivian nodded. "Send them in."

"Do you want me to go?" Marcus asked.

"No, actually, I do not. Lady Pettyfield is not a woman I trust greatly, so I would feel more comfortable if you would stay." She'd barely said the words when the family entered.

Lord Pettyfield was a large fellow, tall and beefy. In his hands he carried his gloves all knotted up in a ball. Behind him came a woman, Marcus presumed the aforementioned Lady Pettyfield, and he could see immediately why Vivian had her reservations. She was also tall, but unlike her hefty husband, she was reed thin and for all intents and purposes rather ugly. But she wore their money proudly—he didn't think he'd ever seen a hat full of so many ostrich plumes, and he was fairly certain one of her hat pins was encrusted with actual jewels rather than the paste ones that most women wore.

She turned and looked into the corridor and her nose wrinkled unpleasantly. "Come, child," she said sharply.

Their daughter entered the room, trying her best to keep her tears at bay, but it was evident from her red and swollen eyes that she'd been crying for quite a while. She looked downward, her previous sobbing causing her to suck in short breaths of air.

Was this the usual scenario that Vivian faced when families approached her for assistance? Marcus was pleased she'd asked him to stay. He might not be able to help with solutions to the problems they presented her with, but he could offer her some measure of protection.

"My lord," Vivian said with a slight curtsey. "What is this emergency?"

"Thank you for seeing us, especially at this hour." It was then that the man's eyes landed on Marcus. "I didn't realize you were already entertaining."

Vivian smiled reassuringly. "No, this is Lord Ashford, a close family friend. Anything you have to say to me will be safe with him as well, I can assure you. He is to be trusted."

Marcus eyed her, looking for any signs that what she'd just said was true. Did she feel she could trust him? Vivian was nothing if not discreet, so it seemed as though she did; otherwise, she would have asked him to leave regardless of her feelings about Lady Pettyfield. She must trust him if she allowed him to stay while another family divulged a scandalous secret.

"I don't think that's necessary," Lady Pettyfield said sharply. She turned her narrow eyes toward Marcus. Her pointed, beak-like nose did nothing to improve her features.

Lord Pettyfield made a sharp cut through the air with his hand. "Enough, Elaine. Miss March is the only one who can help us with this mess," he said. "If she deems Lord Ashford trustworthy, then so shall we."

Vivian rang for a tea tray and had everyone sit so they could discuss things more comfortably. She was so at ease with people. Nothing rattled her, nothing save his words and advances. She remained in control, calm and steady. Once the tea was served, Vivian waited a handful of minutes to allow the family to begin talking.

"I'll need to know every detail," Vivian said when it became clear that the Pettyfields were unsure of how to begin. "I can guess from Elizabeth's tears that this emergency has something to do with her."

"Indeed. The foolish girl has gotten herself compromised," Lady Pettyfield said. "With a duke!" And then she continued to mutter terse words about her daughter, never leaving *foolish*, *stupid*, or *idiot* out of her descriptions.

"I believe I've got an understanding of the situation, Lady Pettyfield. Thank you." Vivian nodded. "I'm certain we can find a solution." She turned to Elizabeth. "I know this might be an uncomfortable conversation to have in front of your family, but I need to know. Did you fully consummate your relationship with this man?"

Elizabeth nodded and sobbed even louder.

Vivian had mentioned to Marcus that some girls had a tendency to do such a thing to get themselves in with a particular man, and essentially ensure their nuptials. It seemed obvious that Lord Pettyfield should have made this visit to the duke in question instead of to Vivian.

"And someone discovered you? Together?" Vivian asked.

"His wife," Lord Pettyfield answered, with another round of insults directed at his daughter.

Ah, so that was why they hadn't called on the duke. Unfortunate, to be certain. Marcus would wager this particular situation was one of the stickiest Vivian had dealt with. It would be interesting to see if she could work her way through this tangled mess.

"That does seem to be a problem." She patted Elizabeth's hand reassuringly. "Might I inquire as to his name, please?"

"Hempshire," Lord Pettyfield said.

"Oh dear, that is a messy situation. He is very handsome and charming. I can see how a girl could be wooed by him," she said for Elizabeth's sake. "But his wife is possessive of him despite his philandering ways."

"Or perhaps because of them," Marcus said.

"She's ruined!" Lady Pettyfield said. "We don't need your explanation of *why* Elizabeth did this, we need a solution. Can she be saved?"

"There is no need to yell or make demands of Miss March," Marcus said, nearly coming to his feet, but he thought better of it and leaned forward. "We are all friends here. If you should like assistance, perhaps you should treat her more kindly, else she might not be able to think of a solution."

There was silence for several minutes after Marcus spoke. Even Vivian looked as if she didn't quite know what to say, but then she sat forward in her chair as if to speak.

Lord Pettyfield spoke first. "My apologies for my wife. As you can imagine we were not expecting the Duchess of Hempshire to arrive at our home last night with our disheveled daughter in tow. To say we're—" He took a shaky breath. "—devastated, well, we're all simply clamoring for what to do to save our dear Elizabeth. There is no doubt that the girl was impetuous and foolish, but it is done now. We can only hope she is not with child."

That statement brought another round of sobs from the girl in question.

Vivian nodded, then tapped one finger to her lips. "I believe I might have a potential solution, but it will take me some time." Vivian came to her feet. "You are welcome to wait here or you may return home and I'll send for you when I know something."

Lord Pettyfield did not even bother looking at the women in his family. He stood and nodded. "If you do not mind, I believe we shall accept your hospitality and stay here for a while. I do not wish to deal with any more visitors at our house today."

"Very well. I will try to do this quickly," Vivian said. She turned to Marcus. "My lord, if you do not mind, I wish you to accompany me."

This was not as challenging or adventurous as crossing

the Tana River full of crocodiles and hippopotami, but he had to admit that his heart rate had increased and he was finding this situation vastly entertaining. Watching Vivian work, manage the families, was fascinating. "Of course." He followed her out of the parlor. "Where are we going?"

"To Viscount Benbrook's," Vivian said.

"Why?"

"We'll discuss that once we're in the carriage."

Not ten minutes later they were seated in the brougham and on their way to Harrowby Street to Michael Benbrook's townhouse. As they rolled down Vivian's street and turned the corner, she met his gaze.

"Michael came and visited with me a couple of weeks ago, after he lost a sizeable fortune in a rather risky investment," Vivian said. "In an attempt to save his family's coffers, he might have instead put them at great risk to lose everything. And they were already in a tough situation because his father had been a poor card player." She shook her head. "I've been trying to think of a way to assist him other than loaning him the money myself. He is a nice fellow, but I fear perhaps a little too trusting."

"You think to make a match," Marcus said.

She gave him a weak smile. "Ordinarily I am not in the business of matching couples. In fact, I've not been a very successful matchmaker to date, but pairing them up does seem an obvious solution for both of them. Elizabeth needs a savior who will marry her and salvage her reputation, and Michael needs an heiress to fill his pockets."

"It is quite a brilliant solution, my dear," Marcus said. "But aside from solving their immediate problems, do you suppose they'll make a good match?"

Surprise lit her features. Her mouth opened and her eyes widened, and then a lovely smile formed as she looked downward. "Thank you. As to them matching, only time will tell, I suppose. But I do know that Elizabeth is the older sister of Lady Richfield. Her name is Miranda and she had a dazzling debut. You know the kind, they launch into society and become, quite simply, the belle of the ball." Her words took on a wistful quality. "No doubt poor Elizabeth was overshadowed by Miranda's success. She married Lord Richfield at the end of her first Season. Meanwhile, Elizabeth has been out a while, four or five years now, and well, a girl who has been on the shelf, as it were, for a while is particularly vulnerable to being seduced by a charming man." Her delicate jaw tightened and she exhaled slowly.

Marcus got the distinct impression she was speaking from experience, not observation. Was that why Vivian was so resistant to his pursuits—because she had been seduced and abandoned?

"Hempshire should be ashamed of himself," she said.

"Most assuredly."

"What Elizabeth needs is a kind man who will be gentle with her, someone who might share her interests," Vivian said.

"And someone who would buy her warm woolen stockings in the winter months," Marcus said.

She smiled shyly. "Precisely. Now, if I can only manage to convince Michael to marry the girl."

At Viscount Benbrook's home, they were met by a

harried-looking butler. He showed them into a parlor that had seen better days. The furniture was old and the stuffing lumpy, and the fabrics were worn and faded. But everything was clean. Michael did not keep them waiting long. "Miss March, I was so hoping I would hear back from you regarding my—" He caught sight of Marcus and stopped.

Vivian smiled and took a step toward the viscount. "This is a friend of mine, Michael. He came along with me today. Can we sit and discuss the situation? I believe I may have found you a solution." She gave a little chuckle and cocked her head. "Albeit a potentially surprising one."

He nodded enthusiastically and sat on one of the wooden chairs, leaving the softer upholstered furniture for his guests. Vivian relayed the story to him and Michael listened intently.

"So there is still a chance she carries his child. It would be a risk," she said.

"But she has a fortune?" Michael asked, his voice hopeful. "Enough to save—to reclaim what I lost, and rebuild?" Evidently he was so intent on salvaging his family's coffers that he was already considering this a viable option.

"A sizeable dowry, and her other sister is already married, so I'm certain we could negotiate a fortune. To be honest, I don't think it would be difficult asking her father for money. He is rather fond of the girl," Vivian said.

Michael was quiet for several moments considering the scenario.

"She is comely," Marcus said. "Pretty in a traditional way, with fair coloring."

Michael winced. "Am I that transparent?"

"No, it is a question I would have asked. If you're going

to agree to a marriage of convenience, sight unseen, it is a legitimate curiosity," Marcus said. "No one wants to marry a troll, even a wealthy troll."

Michael took a measured breath. "Yes," he said coming to his feet. "This will work nicely. I will marry the girl. Where is she now?"

· · ·

Vivian sat quietly in the study with her aunt. Aunt Rose sat at her table building her castle of playing cards. Vivian sorted each piece of mail by type even though it was invitation upon invitation. It was always a tedious process, but today it seemed more so. She would have to send regrets for those occurring while she was away in the country. They were leaving for the countryside tomorrow morning.

She had successfully resolved the situation with the Pettyfields, and though the matron of the family had not been happy with Vivian's solution, Lord Pettyfield had been more than pleased. He and Michael had gone together to secure the special marriage license, and a notice had already been sent to the *Times*. And Elizabeth had finally stopped crying. All in all, it had been a good day—and she'd spent it with Marcus and had enjoyed his company.

It was a marvel, really. Not that she'd enjoyed his company, but that she'd not only allowed him, but asked him to join her. Discretion was extremely important to her, yet she'd allowed him inside two of her families today. It had been a day full of surprises, in more ways than one.

She put aside invitation after invitation to send regrets or acceptance, but at the very bottom of the stack an envelope caught her attention. It was addressed to The Paragon. Vivian felt her blood turn to ice. Something about the print, the penmanship, seemed terribly familiar. She turned the envelope over to find a nondescript green wax seal. With one finger, she popped the seal open.

> *My dearest Vivian:*
>
> *As you may have guessed already, I have returned, my dear, and I see all that you have made whilst I was gone. Such a vast empire of admirers you've created. Remember, though, that I know the truth about how virtuous you are. The Paragon. I truly laughed when I heard such a thing. Your contacts will serve me nicely. Follow my lead, or the world will know who the real Vivian March is. I'll tell them all of your previous transgressions.*
>
> *Yours forever,*
> *Frederick.*

A wave of nausea crashed over her and she dropped the note. *Bastard*.

"What's that, dear?" her aunt asked above her cards.

Vivian had not realized she'd spoken aloud. "Nothing, just thinking about the Duke of Hempshire and his penchant for seducing unsuspecting females."

"Filthy man," Rose said.

"Indeed." But no one, not one man in all of England, was as bad as Frederick Noble. It was not the first time Vivian had been struck by how ironic and irritating his surname was. He was the worst sort of cad.

What the devil did he mean by saying she should follow

his lead? Precisely what did he intend to do with her or to her? She had known the day would come when Frederick would return and she'd have to face him. But she'd often thought that perhaps they could be adults about the situation, laugh about their folly in believing they had once been in love. But clearly Frederick bore her ill will, though why was a mystery. He was the one who had used her and crushed her heart.

This was the worst possible scenario—she was bloody well being blackmailed by her former lover.

Chapter Thirteen

Marcus cut a handsome figure leaning against the hearth as Vivian stepped into Dowager Duchess of Pendrake's parlor. They were to begin dining in another thirty minutes and frankly, she was glad to see he'd decided to participate in at least some of the weekend's festivities. He had not been so inclined when he'd first found out about the house party. She had conveniently left that she'd called upon the dowager duchess and encouraged her to host said gathering, and suggested to whom she should extend the invitations.

Vivian had narrowed down the suitable list of girls for Marcus to court, though he still showed no interest in any of them. As frustrating as that was, she felt certain that being out of London and all the distractions there would help him focus on the task at hand. He needed a wife. Every man needed a wife.

She had also been pleased by the timing of the party, considering the note she'd received last night. Getting out of

London for a few days might provide her some perspective on how to manage Frederick and his blackmail.

She stepped over to greet Marcus. "I am glad you decided to come down for dinner."

He shrugged and gave her one of his far too attractive smiles. "A man has to eat." His eyes slid over the length of her, making her wonder what he thought was on his menu for the evening. "You look rather fetching tonight, though I much prefer the cut of that blue dress you wore the other evening."

"I will not say thank you to that."

He ignored her comment. "Did you invite him, too?" Marcus nodded toward the far end of the room.

Vivian followed his motion and found Clarissa and Mr. Rodale speaking alone in the corner. It was a well-lit area, perfectly acceptable; however, it did appear they were having a rather secretive and somewhat intense conversation. "I have no notion to what you're referring."

Marcus chuckled. "So you do admit to orchestrating this entire affair."

"I admit no such thing." She paused for several moments, continuing to watch the other couple. "What do you suppose they are discussing so heatedly?"

"That I do not know." He took a slow sip of his drink. "You are the one who encouraged their relationship."

"I did not. I merely wanted to smooth over her situation by reminding people that he was a friend of the family." She frowned and looked up at Marcus. "Do you trust him?"

Marcus nodded. "I do. He is a good man, though many will never see him as such because of his birth."

"So you are not concerned for your sister's virtue?"

"No." Marcus released a chuckle. "Justin knows if he puts a finger on my sister I'll kill him. He also knows I would make it hurt."

She was quiet for a few moments, processing what he'd said. He'd lived an entire life in the wilds of places she'd never dreamed of visiting. He'd probably seen more dangers than everyone in the room combined. Marcus Kincaid could be deadly. She knew he'd killed animals to protect people before, but had he been forced to kill another person? She knew that there had been such situations in those countries where dangerous thieves attacked tourists. Marcus jested with her so often that it was easy to forget the life he'd been living.

Such a man could be a powerful ally. She could ask him for help, tell him all about Frederick and his threats, and allow Marcus to handle the situation. How lovely it would be to have someone make something disappear for her for a change. But there was no guarantee that Marcus would agree to such a thing once he learned the truth of her previous relationship with Frederick. Marcus might be so disgusted to learn that she'd lain with Frederick that he could walk away and have nothing to do with her ever again.

"Besides," he said, "I don't believe Clarissa cares for him at all. She still fancies herself in love with that bloke, George Wilbanks."

"I wouldn't be so certain of that."

"Vivian, is something troubling you?" he asked.

She shook herself. It was bothersome, yet somewhat comforting that he could read her in such a way. "No, of course not."

He eyed her for a moment before nodding. "So why are

you not so certain about Clarissa's feelings for Wilbanks?"

"Because I have told you there are many ways in which a woman can flirt with a man." She nodded again toward Clarissa and Mr. Rodale.

Marcus was quiet for a moment as if considering her words. "Are you so certain you can tell when a woman wants to be seduced?"

"Women never want to be seduced." As soon as the words were out of her mouth she knew they were not true. She wished they were. Had wished that for years. But the fact was, were it not Frederick, it would have been some other man. She'd been ripe for the picking and ready, if not eager, for seduction.

She was older and wiser now, but it would seem she still had a weakness for rogues and their wicked ways. As much as she'd like to deny it, she knew she'd like nothing more than for Marcus to leave her no choice, for him to whisk her away in a seduction so thorough, she wouldn't even realize it was happening until it was too late. But she knew that would never happen. There would never be a scenario in which Marcus would seduce her and she wouldn't be a completely willing participant. She couldn't blame him or anyone else for her wanton nature.

"That's simply not true."

"I know," she said, and then walked away.

Marcus had watched Vivian throughout dinner and felt certain that something was amiss. She seemed more contemplative, yet when she spoke to others she overcompensated and was too overtly interested in what they had to say. He didn't think anyone else noticed, but he knew something troubled her.

When they all retired to the parlor for some entertainment, his sister took her place at the pianoforte and played after much encouragement from the crowd. He'd always known she liked music, but he hadn't realized that the music he'd been hearing at their London home was Clarissa. All this time he'd wrongly assumed it was his aunt.

Vivian sat quietly in a wingback chair close to a window overlooking the back garden and the forested area that lined the rest of the property. She held her reticule tightly in her lap and worried the purse's strings.

He moved over to her and stood behind her chair. "What troubles you, love?" he asked quietly.

She sucked in a breath at his question and shook her head.

He leaned closer. "I can tell there is something wrong."

She pressed one hand to her temple. "Headache."

He eyed her for a moment and knew that that would be all he would get from her tonight. Were they alone, he might press the issue, but for now he would leave her be.

"She plays wonderfully," she said of his sister.

"She does."

"Did you know?" she asked, looking up at him.

He smiled. "I did not."

"You did not do a very admirable job of flirting with the women at dinner," she said.

He covered his chuckle with his hand. "I was not aware that flirting was required."

She frowned, clapped when Clarissa finished that piece, then once again resumed clutching her reticule. Another girl, this one Lady Constance Brindwell, came to the pianoforte and Clarissa stood and walked away. When she began playing it was clear she'd had lessons, as had most of the girls in the room, but her skills were crude at best. Vivian winced when she hit the wrong chord. "How are you supposed to court a lady if you do not flirt with her?"

She had him there. Flirting generally was an accustomed form of allowing another person know you were interested in them, precisely the way he'd been with her from the moment he met her. It was natural with Vivian—he didn't have to force it or try to think of something clever to say. He was attracted to her so every exchange between them had become the give and take that went on between ladies and men.

"I flirt," he said.

"When? I haven't seen it."

"My dear, you are privy to it in our every encounter. Perhaps I am not as skilled as I once thought."

She opened her mouth then shut it again. "That is not what I meant, and you know it. You aren't supposed to be flirting with me. It's them. It is why we are here, is it not?"

He smiled. "You tell me—you orchestrated this entire affair. I agreed to attend."

"Must you fight me on everything?" she asked through her teeth. Lady Constance finished her piece and immediately started in on another one. The man sitting in front of them actually groaned.

Marcus looked around the room, at the women sitting there who had presumably been invited simply for him to see if he was interested in marrying one of them. It was a strange way of doing things. Though he wasn't searching for love, per se, he came from a family of men who had all married for love. So looking at these women felt no different than buying a new horse, and it didn't sit well with him.

He needed to feel something, needed to be attracted, and interested, and intrigued—all of those things that Vivian brought to the table. Hell, if he had to marry, why shouldn't he marry her? At least then he'd know he'd be eager to reach his wedding bed.

He should propose to Vivian and be done with this whole matchmaking mess. But he couldn't very well lean over to her now and whisper it in her ear. She'd likely whack him on the head.

The Dowager Duchess of Pendrake stood and walked to the front, where Lady Constance had been making a mockery of the Mozart. "Thank you dear, that will be all," she said to Constance, ushering her back to her seat. "Now then." She clapped her hands once and smiled warmly to all the guests. "I have a very special treat for us all tomorrow. We have been working tirelessly over the last year to restore my late husband's beloved golf course, and I'm pleased to report that we'll all be the first to play it."

Several of the men perked up at the news. One such man cleared his throat, then asked, "Who will get to play first, the gentlemen or the ladies?"

"Oh no, dear, don't be silly. We shall all play together. 'Tis no different than playing croquet together," the duchess said. Then the woman stepped over to the door to speak to her butler who'd entered the room. The rest of the guests began milling about.

Vivian leaned a little to Marcus. "That is a perfect opportunity for you to get to know the girls a little better, perhaps find one you prefer."

"I've already found one I prefer," he said.

Her eyes rounded. "You do? Which one?"

He studied her a moment before answering. She seemed genuinely surprised, but there was something else there, too. Something she hid behind her pleasant smile. If he was lucky, that something was jealousy. "I will let you know in due time."

Her eyes narrowed a little.

The parlor door opened and a woman came in and moved directly to the dowager duchess. "Very sorry to be so late, cousin," the woman said. When she turned to face the room, Marcus realized it was Diana Cosgrove. This could turn into a most entertaining weekend.

Vivian looked up and saw the new guest; her jaw tightened. She averted her eyes from the woman and turned again to Marcus. "You will play golf tomorrow?"

"Let's talk first about Miss Cosgrove," he said quietly.

"Nothing to say. She is a relation of the duchess. It seems reasonable that she would have been added to the guest list," Vivian said.

"She makes you uncomfortable."

She waved her hand. "You said yourself that she does not care for me. Perhaps you don't mind being near people who dislike you, but I find it unpleasant. That is all."

But there was more, he could see it in her eyes. Whatever brief interaction they'd had that night at the ball had been more than a hello. If Miss Cosgrove had in any way threatened Vivian, he would see to it the woman never came near her again.

"About the golf, will you play?" she asked.

"Will you?" he asked.

"I don't believe that golf is my forté," she said. "I should think sitting along the course and watching would be much more my speed."

He considered her a moment, then leaned forward. "I shall make you a bargain, Vivian. I will go and play golf with those other women on two conditions."

"I suspect I'm not going to like this very much." She closed her eyes a moment. "But what are your terms?"

"You must play, too." When she opened her mouth to argue, he held up a finger. "It is always nice to learn new things." He enjoyed tossing her words back at her.

She exhaled slowly. "Very well. And condition number two?"

The dowager duchess went about introducing her cousin, Diana Cosgrove, to the people sitting up front. Marcus took the opportunity to lean close to Vivian's ear, enough so that his breath would warm her skin. "I want a kiss," he whispered.

Vivian dropped her reticule off her lap and quickly bent to retrieve it. She gathered it and excused herself from his side. Marcus looked down at the floor and saw a piece of parchment. He picked it up and stuffed it into the pocket of his vest, then made his own excuses and retired to his room.

Once alone he unfolded the parchment and read the letter.

"Son of a bitch!" She was being blackmailed, that was what troubled her. Why had she not sought his assistance in the matter? He would readily come to her assistance and ensure this Frederick returned to whatever hole he'd crawled from. But she hadn't come to him, so now he had to decide if he should call her on it, ask about this Frederick person, or wait and see if Vivian sought him out for help.

• • •

The following morning, an hour after most of the guests had finished breakfast, they were to head to the golf course that the Duke of Pendrake had created in the last years of his life. The man had been an enthusiast about the game and thus had the course made so he could play whenever the mood struck.

Vivian had never had much interest in the sport, but it had been gaining in popularity in the last several years and she knew many women played as well as men. Marcus was right—it never hurt to learn something new. Besides, if she went along with them, she could encourage him to flirt with the girls, assist them in conversation, and perhaps discover common ground.

She'd do her best to keep her distance from him personally, though, especially when it came to moments of privacy. A kiss. Upon his words last night, her heart had sped and she'd brazenly wanted him to steal the kiss right there in the parlor in front of everyone. This was seriously getting out of hand. Her wanton nature was beginning to take over. She took several breaths to calm her nerves.

She walked through the hall waiting for the rest of the guests to finish readying themselves for the outing. Many of the men had already walked over to the course, and she hoped Marcus had gone on with them. Evidently the rest of the women had decided to all be late.

"Miss March." The whisper came from behind her so

Vivian turned around to the stairs, but found no one there.

"Hello?"

"Miss March." The whisper came again so she walked forward. And then arms came around her and pulled her beneath the stairs. She looked up into Marcus's blue eyes. "It's time for the second condition," he said.

"Not now!" she whispered harshly. But her body betrayed her. Desire surged through her and she wanted nothing more than to press herself against him. "The rest of the party will be coming down these very stairs any moment."

He was so handsome, so dashing that if she thought too much on it, she'd lose her breath. But the combination of his dark hair and those light eyes and the rugged cut of his jaw—mercy, he would drive her to Bedlam.

"Yes, now." He leaned down and placed small kisses along the pulse that flickered beneath her ear.

She put her hands on his chest to push him away, but instead she clutched at his shirt and pulled him closer to her.

He released a low chuckle and made bolder, hotter kisses up the column of her throat to her chin. He nibbled along her jaw, working his way slowly, painstakingly to her mouth.

Kiss me! she wanted to scream. *Do it now before I burst into flames right here.*

As if she'd said the words aloud, he pressed his lips to hers, plunging his tongue into her mouth in a searing kiss. She kissed him back, snaking her arms up around his neck and threading her fingers into his hair. She met his every move.

One of his hands dipped into the top of her bodice and

found her breast. He kneaded it, running his palm against her aching nipple. She moaned into his mouth. He stilled.

"Damnation, Vivian, I could take you right here under these bloody stairs." He held her to him, their labored breathing mingled. He righted her dress, gave her one painfully sweet kiss, then looked straight into her eyes. "We are not done here." And then he slipped out from beneath the stairs.

Chapter Fourteen

Marcus walked out to the golfing area along with many of the guests. Vivian was nowhere to be seen, but he knew she'd keep her promise, that she'd come and participate.

The dowager duchess detailed the rules for those who were unfamiliar and handed out clubs to all the players. Vivian came and joined the group. They'd been divided up into smaller groups so that they wouldn't all be rushing one another.

"Seeing as Lord Greene and his mates have already begun," the duchess said, "we shall allow them to be the first group." She pointed to five people standing to Marcus's right. "You can be second. In fact, begin now as the other group is already several holes ahead."

They moved forward and lined up. The first of them, an older woman whom Marcus knew to be a friend of his aunt's, took the first swing.

"Now then," the dowager duchess said, "the remainder

of you can go together. Remember as you play, you should stay in that same order so you do not lose track of who is winning." She handed the other man in the group, Sir Nicholas Bartleby, a pencil and a small booklet. "You may keep the score in here." She smiled broadly. "Best of luck to you all. I shall see you at the end of the course. I've had lemonade and cakes made as refreshments."

"Thank you, your grace," Nicholas said as the duchess walked off. "We should line up now how we want to play. I should go first so that I can assist any of you who are unfamiliar with the game."

Marcus shot Vivian a look, but she appeared to be listening to Nicholas. "I can go in the last place," Vivian said. "I suspect I'm not going to be very good at this, and I certainly don't want to hold anyone up. My lord," she said to Marcus, "you can go there in between Miss Liddle and Lady Constance. An added benefit of my going last is that I can watch you two men. Consider me a chaperone on this little exercise," she said, but she would not meet Marcus's eyes.

Was that a blush he saw creeping into her cheeks? She wasn't a chaperone. She was in need of one. And she thought to stick him right between those two girls. He didn't think he could stand being the object of Lady Constance's overt flirtations.

"Shall we?" Nicholas asked. "I think the other team is far enough ahead that we can begin."

They all walked together to the course, but then Marcus paused. "I forgot something. Begin without me, I won't be long," he said, and then he left. By the time he returned with a slightly different club, though he didn't think it would make any difference, Vivian was up to tee off, which put Marcus at the very end of their group, directly behind her.

She glared at Marcus and he smiled in return. She chewed at her lip as she focused on the ball, pulled her arms back, and swung. She was a quick study because her ball shot straight toward the hole, only missing it by a fraction.

"Well done, Miss March," Nicholas said. He turned to face her, his features serious. "Are you certain you've never golfed before?"

"Quite certain, Sir Nicholas. Beginner's fortune," she said. "Though I must say, it is surprisingly rewarding to smack something with such force."

Marcus laughed at her remark, but she never glanced his way.

"Indeed," Nicholas said.

When it was Marcus's turn he shot the ball directly into the hole. The women in the group cheered, Miss Liddle going so far as to applaud. "Splendid, my lord," she said.

"Yes, splendid," Nicholas said as they walked to the next hole. He seemed less than impressed with Marcus's shot. "Now then, Lady Constance, would you allow me to carry your club to the next hole?"

The others in their group walked away, making their way to the next hole. Vivian turned to face Marcus. "This is not what we agreed upon," she said.

"I agreed to play golf," he said.

"To get better acquainted with those other women."

He shrugged. "I told you, I've made my choice. I know all I need to know." He picked up their clubs and began following the others. "Now it is merely about the game. Hell of a swing you've got there, Vivian."

Though he could not see her, he felt certain she stood

behind him glaring holes into his back. He wanted to inquire about the letter he'd found, but knew now was not the time. She would flee if he didn't handle the matter just so. He didn't want to spook her; right now he was enjoying her company.

Once they'd joined the others, Constance smiled coyly at Marcus. "My lord, do you think you could assist me? I can't seem to hold this thing correctly," she said, wiggling the club out in front of her.

Marcus was not especially interested in assisting the woman, so when Nicholas stepped forward, Marcus did nothing to stop him.

"Allow me, Lady Constance," Nicholas said. "Forgive me for being improper." He wrapped his arms around Constance and guided her hands to the proper hold of the club. For a moment she looked at Marcus, but then seemed satisfied that some man was paying her attention and turned her focus to Sir Nicholas.

The rest of the game went much as the beginning had. Vivian had excellent power in her swings and got the ball surprisingly close to the hole each time, and Marcus hit it in nearly every time, much to Bartleby's chagrin. It wasn't intended to be a challenging course, so the fact that the man was taking things so seriously was humorous.

They were two holes from the end and Marcus was bored. He would have much preferred to spend the time alone with Vivian.

Lady Constance cried out in pain, bending to grip her leg. "That hurt!" she yelled at Annie.

"Oh my goodness, I'm so very sorry. My skills at this game obviously leave much to be desired," she said with an apologetic smile.

Constance muttered something under her breath that sounded surprisingly like "bitch." Marcus stepped forward.

"Perhaps we've had enough of the outdoors for one day," he said. "You ladies could probably use some refreshments. Sir Nicholas, why don't you assist Lady Constance back to the house and have the housekeeper attend to her injury. I shall escort Miss March and Miss Liddle to the goodies the dowager duchess has waiting for us," he said.

Nicholas straightened. "Yes, excellent plan, Lord Ashford. My lady, shall we?"

Constance still glared at Annie, but allowed the man to lead her away.

"You handled that masterfully," Vivian said to him quietly. She turned to Annie. "Are you all right?"

"Oh certainly. I am sorry I hit her," she said.

"Of course you are. Not a reason for her to behave so poorly," Vivian said.

Annie waved her hand in front of her. "She doesn't care for me." She laughed. "Honestly, she doesn't care for anyone but eligible men." Her eyes rounded. "I probably shouldn't have said that."

Marcus held his arm out to her. "I think it needed to be said. Well done, Miss Liddle." He offered his other arm to Vivian, but she declined, opting to walk beside them. More than likely she was pleased with herself for having finally gotten him to do something woo-worthy to one of his would-be brides. No doubt when he asked Vivian for her hand later this weekend, she would be more than surprised.

It had been several hours since the guests had retired for the evening. They'd had an eventful day and Vivian was tired, but the thought of sleep didn't settle right. She couldn't shake the feeling that someone, or perhaps more than one someone, was here watching her. She'd received that damned blackmail letter shortly before they'd left London, and frankly, she'd thought that being here would clear her head enough to figure out precisely how to handle the matter.

She stepped out onto the garden and was pleased to find that the lights still had some remaining life in them, illuminating her path into the lovely rose garden. She'd come here to find some peace, to soothe her nerves. She missed her morning rides and needed the crisp air to clear her muddled thoughts.

Her morning rides had become her ritual sometime after Frederick had left her. She'd needed something to help her escape. She'd tried alcohol once, not merely one drink, but several. An ill-conceived attempt at forgetting her troubles, an attempt to drown out the constant nagging of the voices in her head. The voices that constantly told her what a fool she'd been, how reckless and well, plain stupid. She never should have given him her virtue, but above that she never should have believed that a man such as Frederick would have picked her above all the other girls in society. She'd been well onto the shelf when he'd begun courting her, already a spinster at four and twenty. Still, he'd been so insistent and so handsome…

He'd been beautiful, looking very much as she imagined Byron had, though he'd certainly not seemed to share the same roguish nature. She should have known. But innocent misses never did, otherwise Elizabeth would not have found herself at the mercies of the Duke of Hempshire.

Perhaps she should write a manual warning the girls of all the signs of rakes. *Never trust a man with lovely curling hair,* she'd begin. *Or a sinful dimple in his chin.* There were so many things she could say to girls to warn them off men like him—not that people would believe her. In order to tell them, she'd have to let them know that she spoke from experience, that she had some authority in the matter. She could never admit to anyone that she'd been seduced, that she'd succumbed to someone's charms.

She took in a deep breath, sucking in the country air with its fragrance and purity. Purity. Knowing what she knew now, she probably would have chosen another man to whom to give her womanhood. Frederick had been beautiful, there was no denying that, but she found now her tastes ran a little differently. If she were choosing now, she would definitely pick someone whom the younger Vivian would have overlooked, but who now consumed her every thought.

The stone bench was chilly beneath her skirts as she sat, permeating the layers of clothing, but she didn't mind the cold. It made her feel alive, reminded her she was still here, and she was still fighting. Whatever it was that Frederick thought he could blackmail from her, she refused to give it to him. The more she thought of him, the more she knew she would have to find another way than to give in to his demands. Perhaps no one would believe him if he told them the truth. She had a spotless reputation in town. He'd been gone for a decade.

Then again, he was a man, and a man from a good family. More often than not, men were believed over women, perhaps even over The Paragon.

"Are you cold?" Marcus's voice intruded into her thoughts, but oddly, did not frighten her.

"A little, but it's nice. Invigorating," she said. Turning toward the sound of his voice, she narrowed her eyes to try to make out his form. His voice came from deeper in the garden, where the light did not reach.

"What are you doing out here?" she asked. She came to her feet and walked in the direction of his voice. She didn't go into the darkness, merely took a few steps closer.

"I was intending to sleep, actually."

"Sleep? Outside?"

"It is not something I've done in London. It's been far too rainy and damp, but here, tonight, it's lovely. The stars are out and the temperature is perfect," he said.

His voice was filled with wonder and excitement and she remembered that this was whom he was. Or whom he had been before he'd returned to England to find himself the new earl and in charge of a sister embroiled in a would-be scandal. He was the man who braved danger to take the wealthiest into exotic locales to show them the animals and the people and antiquities.

"Would you like to see?" he asked.

"See what?"

"Come here, Vivian. Allow me to share this with you, then I shall return you to the garden and you can get back up to your room before anyone is the wiser." He came out of the shadows, his arm extended to her. He still wore his shirt from dinner, but gone was his waistcoat and jacket as well as his cravat. The sleeves of his white shirt were rolled up to his elbows revealing his well-muscled forearms, and the opening at his chest displayed a swatch of his chest. Her mouth went dry.

Without another thought she took his hand and stepped into the shadows with him. His hand was warm, despite the cooler night air and the fact that neither wore gloves at the moment. Now that she thought about it, he never wore gloves. Out of the gentleman's habit, she supposed. It was so easy to forget who he'd been for the last ten years of his life. He'd never planned on being earl, on being his brother's heir.

She'd never once considered that conforming to society's standards might be challenging to him when he'd been spending most of his time in the wilds protecting the same silly people from dangerous animals.

They walked hand in hand deeper into the gardens. Eventually the sweet smell of the roses faded and they stepped off the rock path and on to soft grass.

"Where are we going?" she asked.

"I'll show you."

The moon and the stars shone brightly, giving them some light as they walked across the grounds to the forested park ahead.

"How did you know I'd come outside?" she asked.

"I saw you leave your room."

She turned around and looked at the house and realized she could see much of what was going on in the rooms depending on how much light shone in the windows. "Oh my."

She wouldn't have thought twice about disrobing in that room, but she saw now that unless she stepped behind a screen, anyone out here would be able to see her, just as she was able to see Lord Filmore and Miss Banks in a heated embrace two rooms down from hers. "Oh *my.*"

Marcus chuckled. "Before you begin to believe me an utter cad, that is not why I was down here. I find no thrill in watching fat marquesses seduce ugly women."

Vivian knew it was wrong, but she laughed all the same. It was true. A more unattractive couple you could not have found, which begged the question of why Lord Filmore wasn't coupling with his much more attractive wife. People were peculiar.

Vivian heard the strike of a match and then their hidden space was revealed as light spread around them. He hung the lantern from a tree branch. A hammock strung between two of the larger oak trees swayed lightly in the breeze. He fell into the hammock and it moved against his weight, rocking back and forth. He held his hand out to her. "Join me."

She thought for a moment, knowing full well what this meant, what she was about to do. Could she spend a night with him knowing that tomorrow morning she would continue to encourage him to select another woman for a wife? When he proposed to another woman, announced his betrothal, would she be able to smile and congratulate him? And what of his would-be bride?

She took a sobering breath. Tonight he belonged to no one, tonight he could be hers. Whatever tomorrow brought would be dealt with tomorrow.

Besides, she was already a ruined woman, already a wanton, but this time she'd have a choice. She wouldn't be some lovesick girl with foolish thoughts of romance and happily ever afters swimming in her head. This time she was a woman who knew what she wanted and she was going after it.

She held out her hand and he pulled her to him, knocking her into the hammock and against his body. She released a decidedly feminine shriek, which made him chuckle. But the hammock slowed to a gentle rock and soon she was snuggled against him looking up at the inky sky.

"It's beautiful," she said, her voice breathy and full of wonder.

"Indeed," he said, but he was not looking at the sky. Instead, he watched her face as she gazed at the heavens.

When she realized he was looking at her, she smiled sweetly. "You never give up, do you?"

"Not when I see something I want," he said.

She chewed at her bottom lip. "And?"

"And I want you, Vivian March."

"I'm considering my options," she said with a rather uncharacteristic impish grin.

"Miss March, are you flirting with me?"

"Don't be so surprised. I actually do know how. It is not as if I had to read a manual to share with you all the secrets of modern flirting," she said. "I may be a spinster, but I was a young girl once."

"It becomes you, you know. You should do it more often."

"And should this flirting be with you? Or merely any gentleman whom I might fancy?"

"Only me," he said.

She fell quiet and went back to looking at the sky. Her hand came to rest on his chest, about where his heart pounded. He wanted to ask if she was certain, but he knew she would let him know in her own time. He wouldn't push her. He wanted her to come to him on her own.

Hell, he'd wanted to seduce her since the moment he'd laid eyes on her and remembered her kiss from so many years before. But he'd learned rather quickly that despite appearances, Vivian was vulnerable and he had no desire to hurt her. He admired her, liked her even. She was strong and smart. He had every intention of marrying her now that he'd settled himself on the idea. It all made sense. He knew as well as he knew anything that his desire for her would never wane, which meant he couldn't, in good conscience, marry someone else. But this first time he wanted her to come to him.

"Marcus," she said quietly. She tilted her head back and met his gaze. Her warm, chocolate-brown eyes locked onto his. "Make love to me."

He kept quiet and watched her, and there in her eyes, he saw the certainty. So he pulled her closer to him and kissed her. When he came up for air, he said, "Say it again."

"Make love to me, Marcus."

"I thought you'd never ask." And he kissed her again, taking her mouth with fierceness. He ran his hands up her body and found her right breast. The hammock swayed gently between the trees rocking them as they kissed and as he explored her body.

"You have too many clothes on."

"Remove them, then. Tear the fabric, just please, touch me."

He chuckled. He rolled her to him so he could reach the buttons at the back of her dress. He unfastened enough of them so that the bodice gaped and was easily pulled down, exposing her corset and shift. Through the filmy fabric of the shift he could see her breasts rising above the corset.

"Perfect," he murmured.

"I want you to touch my skin," she said. "I want to touch you."

She was eager for him and the mere thought of her slick folds had him so hard his trousers became painfully tight. "Here, stand up." He came out of the hammock and pulled her to her feet beside him.

While she waited he took the blanket he'd brought to cover himself and spread it upon the ground. "For what we'll be doing, we had to get out of that or else we'd likely pull the trees down atop us."

"I doubt that is possible," she said. Her impish grin was likely the most seductive thing he'd seen. God, she was beautiful. Illuminated by moonlight and the small lantern hanging behind her. Her dinner gown hung off her shoulders, causing the fabric to gape below her breasts. Her arousal had stained the skin above them a pale pink.

"Let's get you the rest of the way out of this dress," he said. "And whatever other contraptions you're wearing underneath." He turned her around so he could see the rest of the buttons. Her hair remained pinned up in the fashion she'd worn earlier that night so it wasn't in his way when he began on the buttons. One by one he unfastened them until the fabric slid down her arms, off her waist and pooled at her feet. He was then faced with her corset.

He'd never found corsets particularly attractive, but with Vivian, he wanted to see her, see everything, not miss one single detail, one single moment. He had her step out of the gown and then he placed it gently on the hammock behind him.

The corset cinched in her waist, accenting her full hips and even fuller breasts. The sight of her standing there in the moonlight in her undergarments was intoxicating, but he wanted to touch her bare skin. Once again, he turned her so he could work on the laces at her back and she released a sigh as he loosened them. He removed the corset, then her drawers and finally her shift until she stood gloriously and unabashedly naked in front of him.

Her chin tilted up and she fidgeted with her hands at her sides. Slowly she turned to meet his gaze.

Her rosy tipped breasts were firm and plump and everything a breast should be. For several moments he simply stared, memorizing every line and curve of her breasts, then he lowered his mouth and covered the tip.

"Perfection," he said. He kissed her then, running his hand down her back to her rounded backside. He gave her bottom a little swat and nibbled at her lip.

He laid her down on the blanket. "Are you too cold?"

She shook her head. "You'll warm me."

Her pale skin, the very color of moonlight, was perfect, flawless. He wasn't certain where to touch her first. "I want to look at you for a moment, take you in." Her legs were shapely and curved in all the right places. Her hips were generous and practically insisted he grab them to pull her to him, but he wasn't done drinking her in. Her waist narrowed, and her navel begged for kisses, and her breasts, ah, her glorious breasts, they were full and beautiful. The areolas were dark, her nipples erect and perfectly pink. He could resist no more. He took one in each hand, weighing them, loving the feel of them in his hands. He kissed the tip of one and then the tip of the other.

"So, so beautiful," he said. His arm snaked around her body and pulled her to him. Now he was wearing too many clothes. He wanted to feel her skin against his, feel her curves, the very feminine bits of her against him. She was all curves and softness where he was angular and hard.

They lay down on the blanket and he kissed her all the while exploring her breasts, her shoulders, her waist, her hips, everything he could reach. He wanted to touch her everywhere.

Chapter Fifteen

He'd told her she was beautiful so many times lately, she was almost ready to believe him. But she couldn't focus on that now because of what his mouth was doing to her body. Oh, the wicked things he could do. Her wanton flesh responded to him as if she'd been created for this very moment, as if her entire life had built up to this night with this man.

Marcus Kincaid.

His tongue continued to move over her sensitive breast until she didn't think she could bear any more and then he sucked her nipple into his mouth and gave her some relief. But then his hand moved down her abdomen to the center between her legs. He splayed his fingers against her, cupping her most intimate flesh.

She waited for the shame and embarrassment to take hold, for the urgency to push him away and flee from this night, but she felt only desire, only the need to be with him right here, right now. They weren't in the house with the rest of the guests; they were here under the stars, in Marcus's world. No, there weren't any snarling lions off in the jungle, but they were here without walls, without limits, and tonight she would be his in every way.

He stopped and rolled off her, and for one panicked moment she thought he intended to leave her, but instead he merely stood to remove his clothes. He toed his shoes off, then unbuttoned his shirt the rest of the way. He removed his trousers and there was not a stitch of clothing underneath.

She gasped.

He looked up and smiled. "I grew accustomed to not wearing drawers during my travels." He tilted his head and gave her a naughty grin. "This is so much more freeing and efficient."

And then there he was, tall and athletic and muscular and so much more than she'd allowed herself to imagine. "Oh my," she said.

He chuckled and crawled back onto the blanket, but this time he started at her feet, kissed both of them gently, then slowly moved up her leg, kissing her shin and picking her leg up to cradle it before his wicked mouth found the tender skin behind her knee. His tongue swirled and his teeth nipped and she gripped the blanket in handfuls trying not to cry out into the night. Up her inner thigh, stopping to bite and tease. She squirmed and moaned and when his mouth found her core, she threaded both hands through his hair. She was a wanton, no denying that. No true lady would allow such behavior and she not only allowed it, she loved it, every tortuous lick and suckle. His moans brought her over the edge and she arched her back as the first waves of pleasure rolled through her.

He continued his sweet torture until she cried out, begging him to give her sensitive flesh a reprieve. He continued kissing up her body as he'd done before. Lavishing sweet kisses along her abdomen, in her navel, across her waist. He nipped and suckled, exploring every inch of her it seemed, just as he'd told her once that he longed to do. Had he truly been desiring her the way she had him?

His hands slid up her torso and he cupped both of her breasts and then his mouth was on them, teasing until she thought she would go mad. She felt the fires flare up inside her, and scorching lust thrummed through her veins. Yes, she was a wanton, but certainly this man was different, special somehow. His mere touch robbed her mind of coherent thought. She felt no shame, only desire, and he made her feel…treasured.

"Sweet, sweet Vivi, you are so lovely," he murmured. He nuzzled her neck and she could feel the hard length of him resting against her core. She wanted him. Now. Inside her. She parted her legs further, but still he continued his maddening exploration of her body.

"You're torturing me," she said.

He chuckled. "Not on purpose, love. I was merely enjoying myself. I thought you too were at least somewhat amused." He moved himself so that the tip of his erection sat at her opening. She tried in vain to push him inside.

"Yes, I am, it is merely that I find myself rather eager to move things along."

This got her a roar of laughter. "Woman, you are the only one I have known that can be simultaneously seductive and humorous." He pushed against her but did not slide all the way in. "Is this what you want?"

She knew it was more than likely disgraceful to ask such a thing, but at the moment she no longer cared. "Yes, please. I want you inside me."

He groaned, a low guttural groan, and then he entered her, filling her up and yet making her crave more all at the same time. She bucked against him, wrapped her legs around his hips.

He kissed her throat, and then he began to move. Deeper and deeper, harder and harder until she thought she'd go mad from the sweet torture. She met his every thrust, gripped his shoulders, closed her eyes and waited for the explosion of ecstasy to rocket through her. She did not have long to wait. The sensation started at her very core and then shattered. He rode her climax until he reached his own, emptying himself inside her with a deep moan.

She realized in that moment that perhaps a wanton wasn't the very worst thing a woman could be.

• • •

The following afternoon Marcus found himself standing in the parlor whilst the rain poured outside. Their hostess had arranged for some parlor games to amuse the guests as they waited for the evening's entertainment, a ball to close out the weekend party. He intended to propose to Vivian that night.

Round tables had been brought in for people to play hazard or whist, but someone had suggested a game of charades might be just the thing.

Marcus searched the large room for Vivian but found no sight of her. She hadn't been at breakfast, either. Perhaps she was simply tired from their night of lovemaking. He had taken her twice more before she'd crept back into her room just as dawn was breaching the horizon.

So here he was in one of the more mundane society functions, but now that he had entered the room, there was truly no polite way for him to make an exit. He could not claim business, as he was not in his own home. Were he a woman he could beg off with a headache, but men never complained of such ailments. He would manage to entertain himself in some fashion.

The charades began. First up was Lady Constance, which did not surprise him in the least. She seemed determined to be the center of attention. She read the slip of paper, smiled broadly, and began her acting.

And it was then that he saw her, seated across the room on a blue and green settee. Diana Cosgrove. He had seen her briefly since she'd arrived, but had yet to make her acquaintance. And, truth be told, he was still most curious as to why she bore Vivian such ill will. There was clearly something between the women, but Vivian claimed to have never even met her. He had no reason not to believe Vivian. It was an interesting enough scenario that he walked across the room and took the seat next to the settee.

He might not be the most mannered of gentlemen, but he most certainly knew how to deal with women. There were plenty of times when wives had come on his adventure tours, following behind their husbands certain of boredom and not looking forward to watching their spouses hunt exotic animals for several weeks. More than once those very wives had wandered into his tent at night, looking for an adventure of their own. He had never been in the habit of bedding other men's wives, though, so he'd flirted and charmed until they'd turned right back around and hopefully gone and crawled between their own men's blankets.

"Miss Cosgrove, I am told," he said smoothly.

Her eyes lit and she smiled. It wasn't a particularly warm smile, but rather more similar to that of a cat's after lapping up a bowl of warmed cream. "My lord," she said. "We haven't been properly introduced."

He grinned. "I won't tell if you won't."

Her smile broadened. "I do like the way you think. How are you enjoying my cousin's little party away from the city?"

"It is a welcome break from London."

"I doubt you truly mean that, but I'll nod nonetheless."

"Miss Cosgrove, I do believe you might be somewhat of a provocateur."

She shrugged daintily. "I do what I can to keep myself entertained."

They both fell quiet to watch the charades. Lady Constance was growing more and more incensed with her movements. People were shouting out their guesses until finally someone hit on it.

"Peacock," Marcus whispered right before the guest at the front of the room yelled it out. Lady Constance smiled and clapped.

"How goes the wife hunting?" Diana asked.

Now, that surprised him. Having that skill at observation could make a person dangerous. He felt it was imperative he discover the root of her dislike of Vivian. If Vivian was to be his wife, he would protect her at all costs and that meant ferreting out whatever problem, imagined or otherwise, this woman had with his would-be bride. "I had not realized that my marital situation was grist for the mill."

"An eligible earl? Of course women talk. It is why we are here this weekend, it is not?" she asked. "Well, not myself, of course, but many of the marriageable women, they are here for you to pick among them."

"I suppose that is true," he said.

"But you are not interested in them, are you?" She smiled, but no humor or warmth lit her eyes. "No, I've seen the way you look at another woman. She entered the room a while ago, and she's been watching you." Diana leaned forward.

Marcus turned to look and there was Vivian near the front of the room. She appeared to be engaged in the charades.

"You are most perceptive, Miss Cosgrove. Do you know Miss March, then?" He could come right out and ask the woman why she bore Vivian such ill will, but he suspected that when it came to Diana Cosgrove, she would be far more honest if he played her little game.

She grinned, but it was almost a baring of her teeth more than a smile. "We have met, but briefly. I cannot say I have the pleasure of knowing her," she said, putting unnecessary emphasis on the word "knowing." "She is a little old for you, wouldn't you agree?"

"I am not concerned about her age—or mine, for that matter. She is not nearly as old as she'd have people believe." Then he paused and they once again went back to watching the game. At the moment Clarissa was doing her best to convince Vivian that because she'd guessed correctly, it was her turn to act out a word.

"You dislike her," he said.

She shrugged. "Ah, you are perceptive as well, my lord."

He wanted to tell her that she had made it blatantly obvious, and had anyone been paying attention, all the world would know of her feelings toward Vivian, but he merely nodded.

"We have a mutual…friend." She waved her hand. "It is of no consequence. I am certain she is a lovely lady. I do not even know her."

"Indeed." He wanted to push her more, but he could tell she had closed herself to that conversation. And she truly had given him plenty of information. Miss Cosgrove and the Frederick who had sent Vivian her letter were obviously connected. "It does not mean that we cannot be friends," he said. He'd always found the old military advice about keeping your allies near, but your foes closer still to be sound.

Her eyebrows rose. "I should like that, my lord."

Clarissa had convinced Vivian to try her hand at the acting part of charades. Vivian glanced at the piece of paper she'd drawn and rolled her eyes heavenward. For a brief moment she met his gaze, then quickly looked away.

"You do not care for parlor games?" he asked Diana.

"Not particularly. I don't see the point in them," she said coolly.

"'Tis what we already do though, if you consider it. At least, most people. Charades," he said.

She gave him a smart smile. "I feel as if you've handed me a riddle, my lord."

"People act out in certain ways to create a perception in others' minds of how we want to be seen," he said.

"Handsome and a philosopher," she said. "Impressive."

"Wouldn't you agree? In English society, in particular,

we're taught from a very young age to act accordingly. We know what behaviors are proper, but to many it is denying their true nature." It was a subtle insult and he'd be duly impressed if she understood it enough to be offended.

"You believe us all to be dishonest, then?" she asked.

"Aren't we, Miss Cosgrove?"

"Please call me Diana." She practically purred as she put her hand against his.

He nodded. "Very well, Diana." So she wasn't so perceptive that she'd caught the meaning of his words.

Someone called out Vivian's word and she was finally able to return to her seat, but she did not look back at him again.

"What you call deception, I believe most would call civilized behavior."

He smiled. "Tell me, Diana, why are you not husband hunting?"

"I have never seen the reason to saddle myself with a husband. I have plenty of money. I have a lovely home. And I take whatever lover—" She paused over the word, allowing her green eyes to roam down his body. "—I choose."

She seemed the wrong sort of nemesis for Vivian to have, but then again, he was surprised by the blackmail. The note had been personal, not bullying Vivian for information she held on some other family, but rather her own secret. A secret that Miss Cosgrove no doubt knew, but he did not. It made for an uneven battlefield, though he doubted Diana would fight fairly regardless. Marcus could easily tell that Diana Cosgrove was not a woman to be trifled with.

Vivian did her best to pay attention to the game of charades, but her mind was focused elsewhere. Last night she'd spent a glorious evening of lovemaking in Marcus's arms and yet the first time she'd seen him, he was flirting with another woman. Blatantly flirting, and in the very same manner he'd pursued her. Perhaps he had played her for a fool and she'd once again succumbed to the wrong man's charms.

Granted, this time was slightly different. She was older now, and knew what to expect. Certainly knew not to allow her heart to get involved. She had loved Frederick, or at least had believed so at the time. But with Marcus, it was pure desire and she knew that. Her heart wouldn't get broken. She wouldn't be that foolish again.

Of course, none of that explained the awful feeling she had as she watched that other woman reach over and put her hand on Marcus's arm. She expected to feel guilty and now she felt the guilt, but she had made her choice.

The woman tossed back her head and laughed at something Marcus said.

"You don't have a guess, Miss March?" Annie, who was seated to her right, asked. "You're so very clever at this game."

Vivian snapped her attention back to the game, but staring in front of her did not turn the thoughts off in her mind. She pinched the bridge of her nose and squeezed her eyes shut.

The older woman to her left patted Vivian's hand. "The headaches happen more and more as we age," she said, as if they were of the same age, even though she had a good twenty years on Vivian. "This charades game is a delightful way to spend time. One would think we would have more of it in Town."

"Oh yes, charades in Town would be lovely," Vivian agreed even though she didn't care if she ever played charades again. "Could you tell me who that woman is with Lord Ashford?" She obviously knew who it was, but hoped the woman would tell her not only Diana's name, but something about her.

The other woman nodded knowingly. "You're right to be cautious. I know you are trying to find him a bride and Diana Cosgrove, while unmarried, would not be a good match." The woman looked around, and then leaned closer to whisper. "She's a most unpleasant woman."

"Unpleasant" didn't begin to describe the heavy feeling that had settled in Vivian's stomach. It was not wariness or caution, but rather an ugly feeling of bone-chilling envy.

Jealousy stemmed from only two emotions: hatred and love. And she knew one thing for certain—she did not hate Marcus.

Chapter Sixteen

Vivian sat in her room waiting for the appropriate time to go downstairs for dinner. She was tempted to send for a tray, beg off with a headache or some such ailment, but decided that would be bad form considering she'd put this whole weekend together. Elizabeth might never forgive her, and she did hate to disappoint people.

So she sat on the stool at the foot of her bed, waiting. She was still angry—angry with herself, angry with Marcus, and angry at her damned realization.

She refused to believe that she loved Marcus. This was simply the same sort of scenario that had happened to her before. A man showed interest and she bared her heart to him. At least this time she hadn't been so foolish as to tell him she loved him. It would pass; it had passed the last time. She should consider it nothing more than a fever. Some rest time, some distractions, and soon enough Marcus Kincaid would be but a memory to her. Though she loathed her mind for going there, she wondered what he was doing right now. Was he seducing Diana Cosgrove as Vivian sat and waited for dinner? Would he smile at her and pretend nothing had transpired? Well, she simply couldn't pretend.

Last night had been one of the best nights of her life. That she would not deny or try to dress up in some other meaning. But she'd be damned if she'd play the fool again. This time while she waited to see if her body carried his child, she wouldn't worry so much as to what everyone thought. She was four and thirty, so what did it matter? No one was going to marry her, so who gave a damn if she had a tryst that ended up in a pregnancy? Hadn't he told her that women her age decided to have affairs all the time? Perhaps if she did carry his child, she would retire from society, for a time.

There was a slight rap at her door. She stood and went over to it. "Who is it?"

The only response was another knock. So she opened the door and Marcus stepped inside.

He pushed her up against the door and pressed himself against her, crashing his mouth down on hers. "I've waited for this moment all day," he said between kisses.

She shoved against his chest, pushing him off her. She had to gather her wits about her before his kisses made her forget what she was about.

"What's the matter, Vivi?" he asked, concern creasing his brow.

"Are you daft?"

"Evidently, as I have no notion as to why you are so angry with me. When you left me this morning, you were in a most delightful mood," he said.

"Yes, that was before I'd realized what a fool I'd been. You seduced me to prove that you could and then once you'd conquered me, you moved on to someone else. What's the matter, Marcus? Did she turn you down? So you had to come back to me?"

"Vivian, what the hell are you talking about?"

"Diana Cosgrove. Did you think I wouldn't notice the two of you in the back of the room, heads pressed together, whispering?" She shook her head. "Is it that you are truly attracted to older women, or do we just present no challenge? We're easy prey for your seductions?"

He shook his head. "I have no interest in Diana Cosgrove, least of all in seducing her. You are a fool if you would think such a thing." He released a tight chuckle. "And you have been anything but easy, love. Is it not clear that I want you, Vivian, only you?"

His words poured over her like a soothing balm, but her mind told her to stand her ground, to keep fighting. Starting an affair with Marcus would certainly lead to heartbreak, and she didn't deserve to be hurt again.

You've survived heartbreak before, a voice reminded her. If she needed to, she could survive it again. Or perhaps this time it wouldn't hurt—perhaps that first time had only been because it was so unexpected and she'd had such grandiose expectations. She had no such notions this time, merely craving the carnal pleasures his flesh could bring her.

Other women did this. Other women chose men to be their lovers, and then when that affair ended, they were free to choose another. She could be one of those women.

So when he reached for her, she allowed him to pull her into his arms. He kissed her and once again backed her up against the door. Before she knew it he'd lifted her, wrapped her legs around his waist, and entered her. He thrust into her again and again, the heavy wood of the door pressing into her back. He kissed her deeply, his tongue tangling with hers.

She knew in that moment, as long as she lived, she'd never get enough of this man. It was a terrifying thought. Her climax rocketed through her and she clung to him as he continued to move himself in and out. And then he found his own release. They stayed in that position a few moments while he pressed tender kisses to her lips and cheeks.

In her mind she heard his words again and again: "I want you, Vivian, only you..."

· · ·

Nearly four hours later, the guests had had dinner and the ball had begun. He had even done his duty and danced with women. Granted, he'd danced with matrons as well as the maidens that had been selected for him. Still, he danced. It was easier to be around them now that he'd made his choice.

This went beyond practicality and desire. Marcus might as well admit that much to himself. He was fond of Vivian. More than fond. What exactly came after fondness he was unsure. But he would wager that Vivian, like most women, would want more than simple fondness when it came to marriage. Even though she spouted that she had no desire to marry, that she was far too old, Marcus knew that was nothing more than a lie she told. Perhaps the lie went so far that she even believed it at times.

He wasn't certain if he'd ever love Vivian the way his

father had loved his mother or the way that Charles had loved his Rebecca, but Marcus knew if there had ever been a woman he *could* love, Vivian was she. And that was enough for him to ask her to be his wife.

So when he found her standing in a quiet corner of the ballroom, he approached. Though she looked every bit the proper lady, he knew the seductress inside. He took her hand to place a kiss on it, but flipped it over, slid down her glove and kissed the exposed flesh of her wrist. She sucked in a breath.

"Dance with me. There is something I wish to discuss with you."

Vivian stared up at him. She couldn't resist thinking about how only a handful of hours before, he'd had her pressed up against her door. Warmth spread through her and she knew a blush stained her cheeks. She opened her fan and waved it in front of her.

He narrowed his eyes and gave her a grin. "Are you flirting with me?"

"No, I was merely attempting to cool myself. It is rather warm in here." She snapped the fan closed and allowed it to dangle from her wrist.

"Dance with me, Vivian."

She inclined her head and he took her out onto the dance floor. Perhaps he was going to tell her which girl he had chosen to court. She appreciated him wanting to share the information with her. After all, this entire situation had been her doing. Still, part of her didn't want to know. But she'd find out sooner or later, and better to hear it from him, she supposed.

She knew it would sting once he committed to another woman, but she also knew the pain wouldn't last long. Selecting a bride for himself would give him a reason, other than his sister and aunt, to stay in England. A reason to finally resign from his position and take himself seriously as the leader of that family.

He swept her into his arms. The waltz moved them across the floor until she nearly forgot about everything but this moment in his arms. Until he'd returned, she'd forgotten how much she enjoyed dancing. He held her too close. There was practically no space between their torsos, and she knew she should protest, but his arms felt too good.

She felt so safe with him, so protected, that she nearly forgot about the blackmail letter from Frederick. Again she was tempted to tell Marcus, to seek his assistance or at the very least his advice on how to proceed, but she was too afraid of seeing disgust in his face when he found out about her past.

"You look beautiful when you smile like that."

She met his eyes. "I had not realized I was smiling." Then she paused for a second before asking, "What do you mean by that? One smile is no different from another."

"Wrong. You have many different kinds of smiles. That one, in particular, is my favorite. It is when you let down that guard of yours, when you forget for a moment that you're The Paragon, and you are simply Vivian. It is a smile unlike any I've ever seen. On anyone."

It was quite likely the single best compliment she'd ever received in her life. And it should have scared the hell out of her that he could so easily see past the charade she'd put on in front of all of these people for the last ten years to the woman inside. "How do you know that?" she whispered.

"Vivian, do you know what a guide does on adventure holidays?" When she shook her head, he continued. "It was my job to not only know the history of the locales we visited, to know how to relate to the native people, but also to watch for signs of danger. You would think that mostly those signs would come from the deadly animals, but it didn't. It was people, thinking they knew better, believing their entitlement crossed oceans and borders and betrayed the laws of the wild. I watch people."

He spoke so close to her ear, she could feel his breath.

Her heart quickened. There was still so much of him she did not know, so much she did not understand. He had evidently been quite good at his post with the adventure tour company, but certainly those survival skills could serve him equally well here in England.

He pulled back slightly so he could face her. No humor lit his eyes; instead, they focused intently on hers, never wavering, just looking at her with raw honesty.

"Marry me, Vivian."

Her heart stopped beating, she was certain of it. Never in her wildest imaginings would she have thought those words would come out of his mouth. Her throat tightened and for a moment she was unsure if she'd be able to speak. She swallowed tears and took a deep breath. "Marcus, if this is where this conversation is going, then the dance is over."

"Hear me out, please. Vivian, there is something here between us. I know you cannot deny it, either. You've felt it. We're good together." He looked deep into her eyes. "So good," he said and she knew precisely what he meant.

"Marriages are not built on that," she whispered.

"Marriages have been built on far less. You must know I care for you."

What he said was true, but it didn't make it right. People did not marry because of carnal desires. It was not something they should even know about one another. If she were a proper lady, she'd have remained untouched all these years.

She became increasingly aware of his touch at the moment. His hand cradling her own, the other pressing the small of her back. She needed to get away from him.

"I thought you would be pleased," he said. "I have come to the conclusion that you are right, that I do need to get married."

Her hands shook and her heart beat wildly. She chose her words carefully so as not to reveal any of her inner turmoil. "I'm glad you finally came to your senses, but I certainly never meant that I should be the woman you propose to. What of all the other girls? Of Lady Constance or Annie?"

"Vivian, do not be dense, love. Who spent the evening in my arms, and earlier today? I have made my choice. Do you honestly believe I would so casually move from your bed to that of another woman?"

Her heart fell to her toes. She stopped moving and he almost tripped over her.

He led her off the dance floor and over to a solitary window by the terrace. She glanced around expecting to find eyes turned their way, but surprisingly, no one had turned to them.

She looked up at him, knowing full well that tears threatened to pour from her eyes. "You have decided that if you have to marry, you will pick me because—because you are pleased with my lovemaking skills?" Her words came out hushed and raw, and she knew any moment she would lose the fight and the tears would win.

"That is only one aspect." He reached to touch her, but she sidestepped him. "I decided that if I must marry, you would be my first choice. I enjoy your company."

She should not be completely surprised. She had behaved the harlot around him. Everything he said was true, but she also couldn't help but notice he mentioned no tender feelings.

"And you believe that this will make a marriage? Marcus, I am seven years your senior. I know that that means nothing to you, but to the people here, the people in London—" She shook her head. "You refuse to see how great a scandal that would be."

"No, what you seem to not hear is when I tell you that I do not care what people think or say. Vivian, if your age does not matter to me, why should it matter to you?"

"I'm sorry, I cannot."

"But—"

She held her hand up. "No. It is my final answer. Go find a younger girl, Marcus. You deserve someone innocent, you deserve a wife whose body isn't tarnished and used." And with that, she walked away.

Chapter Seventeen

Nothing about the evening before had gone the way Marcus had planned. After Vivian had left him in the ballroom, he'd tried to make sense of her words. She had been hurt by his proposal and he hadn't understood why. Still didn't. He'd gone to her room, knocked, but she either hadn't heard it or ignored him. He'd wager the latter, though, based on her reaction in the ballroom.

So it was not until the following morning that he finally saw her again. She sat at the breakfast table talking with Clarissa, and Vivian seemed as she always did, reserved and collected. He couldn't very well speak to her there, there were too many people about. As much as she cared for others' opinions, she'd never forgive him for such a public display. So he waited. But he was not satisfied with her answer.

If she didn't want to marry him, that was one thing. He could accept that. But to insist that he couldn't marry her simply because of her age was an unacceptable reason.

Thankfully they were all returning to London today and he would have more opportunities to speak with her privately.

The butler stepped into the room and walked over to Marcus with a tray. "My lord, this came for you in the post."

Marcus took the letter, noting that it was from Thomas Adventure Tours. He looked up and met Vivian's gaze. "Excuse me for a moment, please."

Then he stepped outside. He found an empty room across the hall. It appeared to have once been a study, but looked underutilized now. He went and stood by one of the windows, popped the wax seal, and unfolded the parchment. The writing he recognized immediately as that of Mr. Thomas's assistant, Mr. Figg. The man had great flourish to his handwriting.

> *Dear Mr. Kincaid,*
>
> *I am pleased to notify you that you have been selected to lead the inaugural Around the World tour that will begin next spring. I do look forward to hearing from you soon, as the plans must be finalized no later than a month from now. We already have several families interested in this exciting new venture. I am in London for the next several weeks, so please stop into the offices.*
>
> *Yours truly,*
> *Reginald Thomas*

He'd been waiting for this letter for so long, ever since Mr. Thomas had announced this trip as a possibility. He'd let his top guides know that it would be up to them to plan the routes and Marcus had used every extra moment he'd had whilst he'd journeyed across Africa to pore over maps and plan everything to perfection. His proposed tour would cover four continents and take an entire year. He had turned in his detailed itinerary, as well as mapped out routes, to Mr. Thomas two weeks before his arrival in London.

He'd wanted this more than anything. Yet today he found little satisfaction in this notice. Even though he still believed in the trip he had put together, he now knew that he was not the man to lead it. Regardless of whether or not Clarissa or Aunt Maureen thought he could lead this family, it was still a task that had fallen to him. He might not always have taken family duty seriously, but until recently he'd never really had to. He was the earl now. There were no other brothers to take this title should something happen to him. He would not leave his family. More than that, though, he realized with alarming clarity, he wasn't ready to leave Vivian.

Marcus read the letter once more and knew precisely what he'd do. He'd simply go to Mr. Thomas and resign, but give the man permission to use his plans regardless of who led the trip. Perhaps he could still be part of the adventures in that regard. He'd been a good guide. He had excelled at survival tactics. Mostly, though, he could manage the aristocrats in a way the other guides could not, because he was one of them. Still he'd loved planning the trips, mapping out the itineraries, and perhaps he could still do that.

"Marcus, what has happened?" Vivian had appeared by his side, her hand resting on his forearm. Such concern showed in her lovely brown eyes.

"Nothing to worry about, love. It is regarding the tour company."

She glanced down at the letter in his hand and took it from him. After reading the contents, she looked up at him. "You cannot honestly be considering this." He opened his mouth to answer, but she continued. "To walk away from your familial responsibilities like that, leave Clarissa unprotected and unmarried, not to mention your aging aunt. Marcus," Vivian said, shaking her head. "You must think about the title you hold now, your duties."

The more she talked, the angrier he became. She didn't have a damned notion of who he was, what kind of man he was. She questioned his strength of character, his dedication to his family, not to mention she seemed to think that he would propose to her one moment and then flee the country the next.

"Actually, I can do whatever the hell I want," he said bitterly. "One of the pleasures of being an earl, I suppose." He ripped the letter out of her hand.

She opened her mouth in surprise.

"One other thing, Miss March. My sister's reputation is my responsibility now, as you so kindly reminded me, so consider our original agreement terminated." He knew that would sting more than anything else he said, and damnation if he didn't want to hurt her. He turned on his heel and left.

Vivian watched Marcus climb the stairs and disappear into the corridors that lined the second floor. She exhaled slowly, trying to piece together what had happened. He'd been angry, furious even. He'd never once spoken to her with any sharpness in his voice, and just now he'd been cold and distant.

She was the biggest fool that had ever lived, of that she felt certain. Not only had she given herself freely to two different men, but she'd lost her heart to both of them. This time it hurt more, this time it felt deeper, more real, and the pain nearly brought her to her knees.

How had she missed that about him? She'd known that initially, upon his return to London, he'd been wavering about what to do with his post with the tour company. But he'd seemed to come to terms with his plight recently and had embraced the idea of marriage, though that certainly had not gone the way she'd planned, either.

But how was it that she managed to select the two very worst men to fall in love with? At least with Frederick she could blame naïveté on her part, but with Marcus, she had no one to blame but herself. She'd fallen in love with a man who couldn't even keep his commitment to his family, and ultimately to his country, considering that his being an earl meant service to the Crown.

Numbly, she made her way back to her room. It was time to finish gathering her things so that she could return to London. She wondered if she could ride back with someone other than Marcus and his sister.

When she stepped into her room she immediately saw the envelope sitting on the coverlet. She recognized that it had contained the blackmail letter, but she felt certain she had left it in her reticule. She went to her purse first and searched through it, but the letter itself was nowhere inside. Perhaps it had fallen out and the maid had placed it on the bed.

She picked up the one from the bed and felt the weight of the seal of wax on the back of the envelope. Not the same letter, but rather a second blackmail note from Frederick. The envelope fell from her fingers. Not only that, but the first one was missing. Her heart pounded so fiercely she could hear it as if it banged against her own ears.

She stood there, staring at the unopened letter, waiting for it to grow legs and disappear, she supposed, but the damned thing simply sat there mocking her. She released a slow breath and picked it up. After unfolding it, she read the words scrawled across the page.

> *My dearest Vivian,*
>
> *You've been awfully busy as of late. Playing matchmaker and companion to so many. It is really quite touching how so many rely on your impeccable reputation to save them from their own sins. What would they all do if they knew the truth about their Paragon? Would they still hold you in such high esteem? Only time will tell.*
>
> *It seems only fair that I should benefit from your skills as well. I know that quite a few of the families you have good relationships with, those who owe you favors, as it were, have ties in the art community. The sorts of ties that could really help someone like me, who clearly should have garnered more success than he has.*
>
> *In truth all the bastards owe me. I should have been able to get into the Royal Society of British Artists years ago on my good family name, but they simply didn't believe I was talented enough. Years in Paris taught me otherwise. Now it is time for all of London to know of my skill.*
>
> *Here are the two families I have chosen for you to approach on my behalf. I should like my own exhibit; a welcoming home to London sort of affair,*

I think, should do nicely. Frederick Noble returns home to share the art that all of France adores. It has a nice ring to it, don't you believe, dear?

I trust your judgment as which of these you will choose for me, but I expect you to contact them directly upon your return from your country party. I am told you are having a splendid time. Do tell Lord Ashford I said hello.

Fondly,

Frederick Noble

Vivian dropped the parchment. "Bastard."

She picked up the nearest thing to her, a pillow, and threw it at the wall with all her strength. It didn't make much of a noise. Fury lit her and set her feet to pacing. She truly was an awful judge of character, it would seem. She glared at the letter lying innocently on the bed, a piece of paper with only words scrawled upon it, yet it held such power. Those vicious words did not seem to be the same sweet man who had wooed her with whispers of love and tender kisses. The fact that she'd ever allowed him to touch her body set her stomach rolling, threatening to dispose of her breakfast.

No! She would not be so easily cowed. If he thought to manipulate her with nothing but a threat, he was mistaken. She had not seen his art in years, but she remembered that he had never been particularly talented. He'd never seen the point in studying with anyone, learning better craft; he just painted something on a canvas and called it a masterpiece. She couldn't stake her reputation on something such as that. Perhaps he'd improved, but still, to go to one of those families and demand they assist him was sickening. There had to be another solution.

. . .

By the time Marcus and Clarissa were ready to return to London, they discovered Vivian had already left with another guest. The two of them had reached their townhouse nearly an hour before, and Marcus had been standing behind the desk in the study ever since. He'd made up his mind about what he needed to do with Thomas Adventure Tours, and he knew it was the right choice.

He needed to familiarize himself better with the family's land holdings and other investments. He wrote out a quick note to their solicitor and requested a meeting with the man first thing on the morrow.

His sister stepped into the office and plopped herself into the chair in front of his desk. He waited for her to speak, but she said nothing.

"Did you need something?"

She eyed him for a moment, then took a deep breath. "Why didn't Vivian ride back to town with us?"

"Perhaps she was in a hurry." He sat in the chair behind the desk and made a note to buy another one. Charles had always been shorter than Marcus and this chair was too low to the ground for him to be comfortable.

"I know you argued this morning, though I could not hear what you spoke of. I know something happened. What did you say to her?"

Marcus leaned forward, bracing his hands on the desk. "Why the automatic assumption that *I* am the one who did something wrong?" He waited for a response, but Clarissa continued looking at him expectantly. "If you must know, I asked her to marry me."

"This morning?"

"No, last night."

Clarissa smiled, but then it faded. "What did she say?"

"She was quite clear she had no interest in marrying me." He shoved his fingers through his hair. "Granted, it was probably not the most romantic of proposals—still, she must know I admire her greatly."

"Yes, admiration, what every woman longs for in a marriage proposal," Clarissa said. "I do not understand your reluctance to admit your feelings."

"What do you mean, my 'feelings'?" Marcus scooted the chair closer to the desk. It did nothing to improve the comfort. "Can a man not find a woman attractive without the entire world thinking him in love?"

Clarissa raised her eyebrows.

Marcus shrugged. "I find her a most attractive woman." He shook his head. Exceptionally attractive. Despite what had transpired between them, he still wanted her. "This is not the type of conversation a man can have with this sister."

"You started this conversation. I only inquired as to your argument." She held up one finger. "Which you still have not answered."

He tossed her the letter. "We argued about this."

Clarissa looked down at the parchment and read the letter. Then she looked up, her eyes somber. "You intend to return to your old position?" she asked quietly, releasing a humorless laugh. "I was only now getting used to you being back." She rounded her shoulders back and sat straighter.

"No, I am not going. I've already written my resignation

letter." He shook his head. "What is it with you women automatically assuming the very worst of me? Have I been so distrustful that you believe my character to be that of a traitor or a thief?"

"Of course not, Marcus." She was quiet for a long while. "She was angry because she believed you were leaving, right after you'd proposed to her."

Realization shot through him. Clarissa was, of course, right. Vivian hadn't merely expected the worst from him; she'd been hurt that he would leave her. "I suppose. It matters not. It is over. I shall eventually find some woman to marry and we'll all forget about Miss March." But could he walk away from her? Knowing he'd hurt her and knowing about the situation she was in at the moment?

"Marcus, you are not going to forget about her," Clarissa said. "You love her. One does not simply forget about their love."

In that moment he had two flashes, one of his father weeping on his knees at his mother's graveside, and then one of Charles holding Rebecca's lifeless body as sobs racked his own. Love—that was what love had looked like to him all his life, the pain after love. And he had run from it. It was why he'd left London to begin with—because he couldn't bear to watch Charles grieve the way they'd all watched their father grieve.

But the fact was, regardless of how he'd run from love, it had found him. Marcus sighed. "Damnation."

"Go to her," Clarissa said.

"I cannot." He eyed his sister. "I relieved her of her duties to help with your scandal."

"Oh, Marcus. What have you done?"

Chapter Eighteen

Vivian had never been to Diana Cosgrove's home, but her address had been easy enough to locate. She took a gamble going there to find Frederick, but she had a sickening feeling that this was where she'd find him. The butler had readily allowed her entrance and shown her into a small parlor, so her instinct had been correct.

The wallpaper and draperies warmed the room in soft shades of butter. The furnishings were not in the current fashion, but everything was clean and pretty. She wondered why Frederick hadn't returned to his family's home. Vivian believed Frederick's mother was still living, but his father had passed away several years ago. His two older brothers were both upstanding members of society, the eldest, the viscount, a vocal member of the House of Lords and the middle son a leader in the House of Commons. The older men of the Noble house were living up to their name.

Frederick made her wait nearly half an hour before he

entered the room. She had to admit, the years had been more than kind to him—he was still, in a word, beautiful. He was dressed more like a poet than an aristocrat, though, which she supposed fit considering he considered himself an artist. Still, now he appeared slovenly, whereas she used to find his dress charming. His hair fell in tousled blond curls about his head, a few falling onto his forehead. His thickly lashed brown eyes looked her over.

"Vivian, darling, I knew you would come." He held his hand out to retrieve her own, but she only looked up at him. "Very well. I see you are not feeling particularly friendly." He sat across from her. "I must admit I am surprised that you have made quick work of the task I set before you. And that you discovered where I've been staying. I understand you met my Diana."

She said nothing, partly because she was still gathering her courage, but also because at the moment the only things she could think to say were horrifically unladylike. She would not give him the pleasure.

He leaned back in the chair, stretching his legs out in front of him. He clasped his hands, letting them rest atop his abdomen. "Tell me which family has agreed to sponsor my exhibit? Lord Harcourt or Viscount Riggens? Oh wait, allow me to guess."

He smiled boyishly and she realized he would never grow up, he'd never mature as a man should, because he was spoiled and entitled and lazy. She did something she'd never before done—she thanked heaven that he'd walked out on her ten years before.

"I should think you would select Lord Harcourt, since his wife is so very fond of artists. Certainly you must have something on that woman, as she must be sleeping with some of the artists she patronizes," he said.

Vivian said nothing and kept her hands tightly clasped together. She had heard rumors about Lady Harcourt, but she had never sought out her services. In contrast, she had handled a situation for Viscount Riggens two summers before, a tiny matter involving his younger son and a slight thieving problem.

She wanted to throttle Frederick. Aside from his obvious handsome features, what had she ever seen in this man? "Neither," she finally said.

His eyes narrowed. "I beg your pardon?"

"I did not speak to either of those families."

He leaned forward, bracing his elbows on his knees. He watched her a moment and then said, "Oh, I see, you had a better family, one I had not considered, with whom you garnered an agreement."

"No, Frederick, I did nothing. I owe you nothing," she said evenly. So far she was managing to keep control of herself. Her voice sounded measured, and she held her hands together to hide the fact that they both shook terribly. She wished she'd told Marcus about this, had him come with her and help her, but that would entail her telling him the truth about her past. Not that it mattered now. None of it did.

His eyebrows rose. "You might not owe me, but it doesn't mean you won't pay. Remember, I know the truth about you." He leaned even further, closing the distance between them. "Vivian, I will have no problem disclosing every detail we shared." He shrugged. "Perhaps I'll embellish a few merely for my own entertainment. Rumors of your wantonness will shock the good families of London."

She swallowed. He was serious, she knew that much. Still, it mattered not. She would not use her clients for this man because she knew one thing for certain—once she gave in to his requests, once she said yes, it would never end. She'd be beholden to him for the rest of her days, and nothing was worth that. She wanted him out of her life for good.

She came to her feet. "I said no. You do what you must." She took a deep breath. "But remember that to the people in London, I am The Paragon." She tilted her head up. "They look to me for guidance. You have been gone for a decade and you've seemingly made nothing of yourself. No one will believe what you say about me." She knew that probably wasn't true, but she'd be damned if she let him know that. "I came here to tell you that."

"You will regret this, Vivian. You mark my words." He stood and pointed at her. "I will make you regret this."

"I have many regrets where you're concerned, Frederick, but I guarantee, *this* will not be one of them."

• • •

Had the request to attend that night's ball come from anyone but her Aunt Rose, Vivian would have begged off. But the ball was at Rose's dear friend's home and her aunt hadn't wanted to attend alone. In addition, Vivian knew she needed to be out among people. This was her life, these people were her friends—or at the very least her clients and acquaintances.

Vivian stood in the ballroom doing her best to appear pleasant, but it was a struggle. All she really wanted to do

was go home and have a good cry. It took all her strength
to maintain her facade. She had no idea what Frederick was
going to do or when he planned to do it. For all she knew, the
rumor, or rather the truth about her, already spun through
the room.

She did, however, know that Marcus was here. She'd seen
both Lena and Clarissa when she'd first arrived. Clarissa had
merely hugged her, then walked away with tears heavy in
her eyes. Vivian had no idea what that had been about. Lena
had asked about their weekend trip, but Vivian had been
vague and then thankfully her aunt had come by and asked
her to come meet a friend's cousin who was in town visiting.

After that interaction Vivian had found a quiet corner
to stand in from which she could merely observe the goings-
on. And this was where she'd been for the last four songs the
band had played.

She'd wanted to talk to Lena, but hadn't known what
to say. For the first time, she'd felt part of someone's family.
Between Lena and Clarissa, Vivian had felt as if she'd
belonged, and it was odd because she'd never felt that way
with any of the other families she'd worked with.

A stir began over by the French doors that led out onto
the terraces. More and more people left their dancing and
their refreshments and gathered in that direction, until the
entire crowd in the ballroom had gone outside. The band
stopped playing, and servants scuttled about. Outside, the
voices rose. A few women screamed.

Vivian made her way outside and searched the crowd
for her aunt. She found her leaning against the balustrade,
looking upward.

"Aunt Rose, what is all the commotion?" she asked.

"I can't see much from here, but from all the mutters, I'm to believe there is someone who has climbed out onto a third-story balcony and is threatening to jump," Rose said. "Quite tragic."

"I'll try to get closer," Vivian said. She pushed her way through the crowd. Once she'd made her way down the steps to the grassy garden area, she asked a gentleman, "Who is it?"

"Someone up there," he said, pointing to the top story of the house. A person stood in the rounded balcony that probably belonged to one of the bedchambers. "It's a woman."

Vivian followed his pointing hand, looking upward, and sure enough there was a woman standing on the circular stone balcony. The woman's cloak billowed behind her, blowing in the wind. "Who is that?" Vivian asked, but to no one specifically.

The crowd continued to murmur, a few people yelled up to the girl. She peered over the edge of the balcony presumably looking at the ground beneath her.

"Annie Liddle." The name began to make its way through the crowd.

"Annie," Vivian said quietly. She hadn't known the girl very long and didn't know her well, but out of all the women she'd suggested Marcus court, Annie had been Vivian's favorite. She was a sweet girl, funny and charming, but something had obviously gone terribly wrong.

Vivian moved through the crowd, angling for a place where she could better see the girl, and in the process she ran right into Marcus.

"What the devil is going on?" he asked.

Vivian pointed. "That's Annie."

He looked up and cursed. "What is she doing up there?" But it was a question that required no answer. "There's got to be a way to get her down."

By now her parents had gathered and were yelling things up to her, words of love and encouragement, but her mother was sobbing so loudly no one could decipher her words. "Annie, you get down here right this instant," her father said sternly, obviously trying a different technique to convince his daughter to leave her perch.

"I can see clearly up here, Mama," Annie said. Her voice silenced the crowd. "Everything makes sense now."

"What are you talking about, girl? Come down and we can discuss it together," her father pled. "Please, Annie, look at how your mother weeps for you. Do not do this to her."

"Mama, do not be sad, it will all be over soon." Annie released a haunting laugh. "Tears solve nothing. You told me that, remember, Mama?"

"I'm going up," Marcus told Vivian. "I'll try to pull her back inside."

Vivian nodded, and then grabbed his arm. "Please be careful."

She moved further into the open space where she could best see Annie. There she found Annie's younger sister, Cynthia, sobbing next to her parents. Vivian put her hand on the girl's arm. She couldn't have been more than eighteen years old. "Do you know why she's up there?" Vivian asked her.

The girl nodded. She swallowed and glanced at her parents, but they were still both focused on Annie. "He left her."

Vivian frowned. "Who? Who left her?"

"Samuel. They were in love, but father forbade it because Samuel did not come from a good enough family." Cynthia swiped at her tears. "Annie told Samuel she'd follow him anywhere. She told him that it didn't matter to her what our parents said, but Samuel didn't want to wait, so he left her. Went to America to find his fortune, he told her. Said there was no place for her with him," Cynthia said.

"So she is heartbroken," Vivian said more to herself than Cynthia. Vivian certainly knew how that felt, and though she'd never contemplated suicide, she knew how desolate it could feel when your whole world crumbled atop you. How had they not seen this with Annie at the party this past weekend? They'd been with her, had played golf and charades and she'd seemed in jovial spirits.

"And ruined," Cynthia added.

The words seemed to echo all around Vivian as if Cynthia said them again and again. Vivian watched the scene unfold before her almost as if she wasn't even in the same garden as the people surrounding her. The crowd behind her disappeared.

Ten years ago this could have been her. She could have done something drastic rather than swallowing the secret and hoping no one ever found out. Hell, she hadn't merely swallowed it, she'd built her entire life around it, burying it a little deeper with every decision she'd made since then. But it was no different than her aunt's card houses. Vivian knew it was finally time to pull out that bottom card and allow the other cards to fall where they may.

Vivian took a step forward. "Annie," she called out. "Can you hear me?"

"Miss March," Annie's voice caught on a sob. "Is that you?"

"It is, dear."

"It's beautiful up here," Annie said, her voice sounding fragile and strange.

"I'm certain it is. I'd wager you could see much of the city from up there during the daylight," Vivian said.

"Yes, I can see the lights from across the Thames even now," Annie said.

"I want to tell you a story, Annie. Will you listen to it before you—" She paused, grappling for the right words. "—before you make any decisions?"

"This is not the time for stories," her father said harshly, but Cynthia grabbed his arm and pulled him back.

"Let her, Father," she said gently.

"Annie, are you listening?" Vivian asked.

"I don't have much time left," Annie said.

With everything she said it was as if she became more and more distant.

"I'll talk quickly, then. Did you know that I was in love once, too?" Though she left out the part about knowing now that there was no real love to be found with Frederick, it had been nothing more than young obsession and love—the ideal of love.

"Yes, I was in love with a man named Frederick Noble and, well, he told me he loved me as well." Vivian ignored her own tears as she spoke, allowing them to fall freely. What people thought of her no longer mattered. All Vivian cared about at the moment was keeping Annie safe. "We planned to marry. He was gentle and charming and so adoring. He promised me so much. So many promises. One day, because I believed we would be married, because I believed his promises, one day I gave him my virtue." Vivian ignored the gasps and murmurs that ran through the crowd.

"I gave him everything, Annie, my heart, my body, all because I believed what he told me, believed that we would marry, that he loved me. And then on the very night when he was supposed to propose, he left. He deserted me with nothing more than a letter sent to my house. A letter with more empty promises." Vivian shook her head, remembering the cruelty of the man she'd given herself to.

"I was devastated. Heartbroken and terrified, Annie, perhaps similar to the way you're feeling right now. I was so frightened someone would discover the truth—that my aunts would find out my secret. I never wanted to disappoint them. I knew I'd been ruined. Knew I was not fit for another man. So I told no one. I buried the secret and built my entire life around it."

Vivian turned and made a sweeping motion to the crowd behind her. "I hid my secret and then worked to hide all of theirs. Oh, the things I know about the people in this town."

Vivian could see Marcus coming up behind the girl, and she took a steadying breath. Annie was almost safe. But there was more she wanted the girl to know.

"And all these years, I thought I was safe. Frederick hadn't returned, he'd stayed in Paris and my secret was mine to protect. He has come back to London, though, not too long ago, it would seem, and with him he brought wretched letters and threats, blackmailing me to protect my secret."

Again, more shocked gasps whispered through the crowd.

"But protecting that secret isn't worth it, *he's* not worth it. I made a mistake. You made a mistake, but it doesn't have to destroy your entire life." Vivian glanced at Marcus. "You could still know love, still go on to do everything you always planned to do." She glanced at the people all around her. "Look at all the faces out here, Annie. If you knew how many other women in this crowd had done the very same thing you have done, you would be far more forgiving of yourself."

Annie stood there for several moments and then she nodded. She turned back to the window and Marcus appeared offering a hand to assist her back inside.

The crowd cheered. Vivian stood waiting for Marcus to bring Annie down. A handful of people, starting with Annie's parents, thanked Vivian, but for the most part people stayed clear of her. Perhaps tonight she had gone from paragon to pariah, but at least she had done it on her own terms and hadn't allowed Frederick the pleasure. And if she were completely honest with herself, she was glad she'd told them all, in her own words. She was glad the burden of that secret was gone.

She felt lighter, perhaps ready to start anew. Marcus came out of the house with Annie and walked the girl straight over to her parents. Annie embraced her family, but one look at Vivian had her rushing into Vivian's arms.

Vivian caught Marcus's glance above Annie's head. His jaw clenched and the steely look in his blue eyes seemed to grab hold of her heart. Then he turned and walked away. Vivian closed her eyes and held onto Annie.

"Thank you," Annie whispered. "I thought I was so alone."

"Of course not," Vivian said, rubbing the girl's back. "Perhaps we could start a club," she teased. But inside, Vivian felt as if she were the one dying. Marcus had heard the truth about her and been so disgusted, he'd walked away.

Once Marcus had gotten Annie safely back down to her family he taken one look at Vivian and wanted nothing more than to pull her in his arms and hold her tight. But he had more pressing matters to deal with first. He would go to her soon, tell her what an ass he'd been by storming off the way he did. He'd had no idea about the burden she'd been carrying, or why that son of a bitch had been blackmailing her, which was precisely why he had someone to see before he went to Vivian, now that he knew the man's name.

Marcus felt certain he knew right where to find him. Now everything made sense.

Vivian's reaction to his letter from the tour company made sense now. She'd thought that after he proposed he was going to leave her exactly the way Frederick had. And she hadn't seen herself as worthy of being another man's wife, since she believed herself to be tarnished. *Oh sweet, sweet, Vivi.*

Upon his arrival at Diana Cosgrove's townhouse, he slammed the knocker against the door. The butler had barely opened it before Marcus shoved the man aside. He tore up the stairs and opened several bedchamber doors before he found her. Diana lounged on her bed, the coverlet half covering her, half not. She didn't seem to care much that she was exposing herself to him.

"Where the hell is he?" he asked. Marcus looked around the room. The wall across from the bed held a dressing table with the usual accoutrements. Leaning next to the table and against the wooden paneling were several painted canvases.

There was a door in the far right corner, presumably leading to a dressing closet or adjacent room. He looked back at Diana.

She gave him a slow smile. "Whom are you looking for?"

"Darling, I was thinking—" Frederick walked through the doorway from the adjoining room without a stitch of clothing on him. "Ah, Lord Ashford, how interesting of you to join us. I should think you would allow us to dress properly before we can accept visitors. We could meet you in the parlor on the first floor."

"This won't take long," Marcus said. With that, he slammed his fist into Frederick's perfect face. "And it certainly doesn't require clothes on your part." He landed another blow and then another. He wanted to continue to hit the man until all the anger he felt on Vivian's behalf seeped out of his body, but he knew if he did that, he'd kill the man.

Frederick howled in pain and Diana screamed. Marcus stepped away from the man who'd doubled over in pain. Frederick looked up at him, blood pouring from his now broken nose and Marcus noted the bastard would probably be nursing some cracked ribs. "You broke my nose," he said.

"If either of you two ever contact Miss March in any capacity, you will have to deal with me. Am I understood?"

"Now see here, man," Frederick said, coming to stand upright. His voice was nasal as he continued to hold his bleeding nose.

"No, I will not see here." He took a step toward Frederick and the man backed up. "Allow me to put it into terms you can readily understand. I have spent the last ten years of my life traveling through the wilds of Africa and India. I have seen men killed in ways in which the civilized people here in

England could never even dream." He met the man's eyes. "Don't make me have to come find you again. The next time I will not be so kind."

Frederick nodded swiftly.

Diana slid from the bed and now having found some shred of modesty, she clutched the coverlet to her body. "What of your art, dearest? That bitch owes you."

Marcus whipped towards her. "Is that what he told you?" Marcus shook his head in disgust. "No, he seduced her while she was still an innocent, stole her virtue, and then broke her heart. Vivian owes him nothing." Then he looked back at Frederick and motioned to the paintings leaning against the far wall. "And you are a terrible artist. No one in London will ever pay money for your wretched paintings."

...

Vivian sat at her dressing table absently braiding her hair. So much had happened in the last few weeks it was hard to think upon all of it at once. Tomorrow everything would be different. She would no longer be The Paragon. People would no longer seek her out to give them coverage and sanctuary. She had ruined everything by sharing the truth about herself tonight. Now everyone knew of her less than virtuous past.

She searched her mind and body for signs of guilt or regret, but oddly, found none.

She had even received a note from Annie this evening thanking her for sharing her story, for stopping her from doing something so profoundly stupid.

The carriage ride home had been spent with Aunt

Rose crying into her embroidered handkerchief. She hadn't been upset with Vivian for her mistake, but rather for her believing that she or Lillian would have ever seen Vivian differently because of it. Vivian had apologized, but knew that tomorrow she'd have to talk to her more. Vivian owed her more of an explanation.

Suddenly her door opened and Marcus stood there.

"Marcus, what are you doing here?"

But then he was there, right next to her, his hands all over her, his mouth on hers, and words were forgotten in the kiss. He threaded his fingers through her damp hair, unbraiding it and allowing the whole of it to cascade down her back. He massaged at her scalp, then his fingers moved to the fastenings on her nightrail. So deft were his movements, the only way she knew he was done was the cool air hitting her bare skin as the garment fell to her feet.

Then his mouth was on her breast, sucking and nipping and devouring. He seemed to be everywhere at once, touching her, kissing her, moving her toward the bed. A moment later he was undressed and atop her. His body was warm and heavy on hers and so very welcome.

She thought she'd lost him, but he was here, in her bed. She gave her heart permission to hope.

She could be here in this moment forever, having him press kisses all over her body, having his fingers weave magic through her veins. Just him. Just Marcus and she could be happy. Finally happy because she loved him. It was on her lips to tell him and then he was inside her and she forgot everything but the sensations he created.

Her body matched his movements, with every thrust she met him, climbing higher and higher until her climax teetered at the edge of the cliff. She bucked against him, trying to push herself over, to release herself from the sweet torture. Her nails dug into his shoulders and she wrapped her legs around his waist. And then her release hit and she pushed her head into her pillow and moaned his name again and again.

They lay quietly a moment. He rolled off her and settled himself on the pillow beside her and then he pulled her to him. She put her head on his chest, listening to the steady rhythm of his heart. In that moment she realized none of this would be worth it if she couldn't be with Marcus forever. Letting herself love Marcus would bring her peace and make her whole. Most of all, she deserved to love him. She deserved for him to love her in return. That is, if it wasn't too late.

"I love you," she said.

He pulled back until she could see his face. "What did you say?"

"I said I love you. Marcus, I love you."

His eyes narrowed. "What is this about, Vivian?"

"Us. Me." She released a nervous laugh. "It's about what I want. I want you." She eyed him for a moment, trying to gauge his reaction, but he was quiet. She chewed at her lip. "Is that question you asked me the other day…" She exhaled slowly. "Do you still want me? Do you still want me to be your wife? Because I would very much like another chance to answer."

"Yes, I do, but what about Thomas Adventure Tours?" he asked.

She shook her head. "I'll go with you. I could probably stand to get out of London for a while." Then she narrowed her eyes at him. "But something tells me that's not really what you're asking me. You are resigning," she said as she realized what a fool she'd been. "Oh, Marcus, I'm so sorry for accusing you."

He squeezed her to him. "Perhaps we shall travel someday, but yes, I resigned, you goose. I couldn't bear the thought of leaving you, which, frankly, is not very masculine of me."

She smiled broadly as happiness poured through her like rays from the sun, warming every part of her body. "I won't tell anyone." She waited for him to say something else, but he was quiet. "I am sorry I said such nasty things to you about that, Marcus." She shook her head. "I do not think such things about you."

"You don't need to apologize for anything. Vivi, I wish you'd told me about the blackmail. I could have helped. I found the letter, you know, but I waited, like a fool, hoping you'd seek my help."

She released a shuddering breath. "I didn't want you to know the truth about me."

"The past is the past. I never give that a second thought. But I doubt you'll ever hear from Frederick or Diana Cosgrove ever again."

She leaned on her elbow and eyed him. "What did you do?"

"I might have hit him. Once or twice."

"Marcus," she chided, then giggled. "Did you hurt him?"

"Broke his nose."

She kissed him firmly on the lips. "Oh, he'll hate that. He loves his face." His blue eyes locked on hers. "Thank you." She was quiet for a few moments before asking, "Does that mean…?"

"What?" he asked. "Ask me, Vivi."

"Does that mean that you love me, too?"

"Yes, you maddening woman, I love you."

"No matter what?"

"No matter what."

Epilogue

CHRISTMAS, 1866

Vivian stood in front of the tree in the corner of their parlor and tilted her head. The clean piney smell from all the hung boughs filled the air. She inhaled, enjoying the distinctive holiday smells.

She eyed the tree. Something was still missing. Marcus had already put candles all over the evergreen, and now she was putting on the finishing touches. Perhaps it needed a few more ribbons. She bent to retrieve them, and a fluttering moved through her belly. She stood abruptly, hand to her rounding abdomen. There—against her hand, she felt it again, a slight movement. Tears sprang to her eyes.

"Hello in there," she whispered.

"Who are you talking to, love?" Marcus asked from the doorway.

"The baby. Come here, he's moving."

"Still so certain it's a boy?" he asked, striding toward her.

She grabbed his hand and put it on her stomach. "Right there, feel that?" Another movement. She smiled broadly at her husband. "He's strong."

"Yes," Marcus said. "But *he* might be a *she*."

"You know you are supposed to want an heir."

He shrugged and gave her one of those grins that still made her heart flip-flop. "I do, but perhaps this first one could be a little girl. A girl as beautiful as her mother, who will smile up at me with those same brown eyes, and I know already I shall be defenseless."

She grabbed Marcus and fell into his arms for a tight hug. "I love you so very much."

He squeezed her to him. "And I love you." He kissed the top of her head. "I brought you something." He led her to the settee and made her sit. "Besides, you should be resting. I can finish decorating the tree."

She looked over at the tree in the corner. It still seemed too bare in some spots. "It needs more color. It needs to be finished before the rest of the family arrives in a few short hours," she said.

He came over with a beautifully wrapped package and set it in her lap.

She looked up at him. "But Christmas isn't until tomorrow."

"An early present," he said. "Open it." He sat next to her on the settee.

Love swelled within her, threatening to choke her, and she wondered for a moment if anyone had ever died from too much happiness. She carefully unwrapped the paper, and then opened the box. Inside she found three pairs of warm woolen stockings. Tears filled her eyes and she ran her fingers down the length of them. They were soft, the finest of wools, and they must have cost him a fortune.

"Yes, this, this is precisely what I always dreamed of. I just didn't know it would be you," she said. She met his gaze, startled by his handsomeness and the love that shone in his eyes.

"It's merely stockings, love," he said, smiling.

"No, it's so much more. *You* are so much more. I love you."

"But it is everything you deserve. I love you, Vivian." Then he kissed her.

OTHER BOOKS BY ROBYN DeHART

THE FORBIDDEN LOVE SERIES
A Little Bit Sinful
A Little Scandalous

THE MASQUERADING MISTRESSES SERIES
No Ordinary Mistress
For Her Spy Only
Misadventures in Seduction

Undercover with the Earl

About the Author

As a life-long lover of stories and adventure, it was either become a stuntwoman for the movies or live out those adventures from the safety of her PJ's and computer. Award-winning author, Robyn DeHart chose the latter and couldn't be happier for doing so. Known for her unique plotlines and authentic characters, Robyn is a favorite among readers and reviewers. Publishers' Weekly claims her writing to be "comical and sexy" while the Chicago Tribune dubs her "wonderfully entertaining." Robyn is also a four-time RT Bookclub Reviewers' Choice award nominee, and a three-time RomCon Reader's Crown nominee. Look for two new series coming from Robyn in 2013. Robyn lives in Texas with her brainy husband, two precocious little girls, and two spoiled cats. You can find Robyn online at her website or at one of her group blogs, the Jaunty Quills or Peanut Butter on the Keyboard.